The Lost Foal Mystery (Young adult horse fiction)

A Teen Horse Adventure of Friendship, Secrets, and a Race to Save a Missing Foal

The Saddle Creek Riders

Book 2

Wren Willowbrook

Chapter One

Emma Carter woke before her alarm. The sky outside the window was still a deep bluish grey, the kind of early morning color that felt more like night than day, yet her body was already buzzing with the same excitement she had felt since moving to Saddle Creek Ranch. It had been only a few weeks since her first riding show with Willow, but the memory still glowed inside her like a warm lantern. She stretched beneath her blankets and listened. The house was quiet except for the soft hum of the refrigerator down the hall and the occasional ticking from the hallway clock.

She rolled onto her back and stared at the ceiling. Something felt different this morning. A strange prickling sensation, like the air itself was holding its breath. She tried to shrug it off. Plenty of mornings felt mysterious on the ranch, especially before sunrise. Sometimes it was fog drifting low over the paddocks, and sometimes it was the distant call of owls or the groan of a shifting barn beam. Ranches had their own kind of music. Emma was still learning all the notes.

She slipped out of bed, tugged on her jeans and a warm hoodie, then pulled her hair into a loose ponytail. Her boots thudded softly on the wooden floor as she crept to the kitchen so she would not wake her aunt and uncle. Aunt Sarah had been working late at the diner the night before, and Uncle James liked to let her sleep in on her days off. Emma poured herself a quick glass of orange juice and grabbed a banana. Her aunt always joked that Emma was starting to run on horse time instead of human time.

She stepped outside and closed the door gently behind her. The cold morning air wrapped around her face and hands, clearing her mind instantly. The ranch spread out before her in sleep-drenched stillness. Only the faintest sliver of sunrise showed on the horizon, like the world was just beginning to think about waking up.

Gravel crunched softly beneath her boots as she made her way toward the barn. The familiar smell of hay, cedar, and horse lingered in the air. She breathed it deeply, letting it settle inside her like something safe and steady. Willow would be waiting for her. The chestnut mare always grew restless when Emma took too long to arrive, even though Emma fed her at the same time every morning.

But as Emma neared the barn, something made her pause. Willow was not the only one awake. A low ripple of movement drifted from inside, soft and uneven. She stepped closer. The mares were shifting in their stalls, not just stirring lazily the way they usually did, but pacing at the edges, snorting, and flicking their ears toward the woods behind the barn.

Emma frowned. Horses did not act like that for no reason.

She ducked inside the barn and almost bumped straight into Riley.

Riley stood in front of Storm's stall with her arms crossed and her blond hair shoved messily into a bun. Storm, her grey gelding, stamped a hoof anxiously. Riley lifted her eyebrows as if she had been caught doing something embarrassing.

"You're early," Riley said.

"So are you," Emma replied.

Riley huffed. "Storm woke me up. He kept pawing at the stall door. You would think he heard a ghost or something."

Emma walked past her and peeked into Willow's stall. The chestnut mare lifted her head sharply, eyes wide and alert, nostrils flaring in the direction of the woods. Her muscles twitched with tension, something Emma had only seen a few times, and always when Willow sensed something unusual.

"She's nervous," Emma murmured. Her voice dropped without her meaning to.

Riley walked over. "All of them are. I checked the paddock and did not find anything. Maybe a coyote came too close again."

But Emma shook her head slowly. "Willow is not scared of coyotes. She just gets protective. This feels different."

Riley did not argue, but she did not agree either. She just shifted her weight to her other foot and let her eyes drift toward the barn doors.

For a long moment they both stood still and listened. The barn creaked in the morning chill. A few horses shuffled. A faint wind rustled the leaves outside.

Then Emma heard it.

A sound so soft it almost blended into the rest.

A faint, thin cry. High pitched. Almost like a whinny, but not quite.

More like something calling for help.

Emma straightened. "Did you hear that?"

Riley hesitated, then nodded once. "Probably a bird."

"That was not a bird."

The cry came again, this time slightly louder, as if whatever was making it was struggling.

Emma's heartbeat quickened. She took a step toward the barn doors. "It came from the woods."

Riley reached out and caught her sleeve. "Hold on. Let me think."

But Emma was done thinking. Something needed her. She could feel it. She tugged her sleeve gently out of Riley's grip. "We should check."

"With no adults?" Riley asked, her voice sharp. But there was a flicker in her eyes that looked more like worry than annoyance.

"Just to see."

Riley sighed and then grabbed a flashlight from the hook near the stalls. "Fine. But I am telling Dale if we get eaten by a bobcat."

Emma tried not to smile. Riley pretended to be annoyed, but she never let Emma go into the woods alone. That had become its own quiet rule between them.

They stepped outside. The cry did not come again immediately, but Willow pushed against her stall door as if urging them to hurry.

Emma's breath puffed in the air as they walked toward the edge of the woods. The light grew brighter by the minute, though the sun was still hidden behind the rolling hills. A soft fog curled low along the ground, making every tree look taller and darker.

They followed a narrow trail that wound through the back pasture and disappeared between the pines. Dew clung to Emma's boots and the hem of her jeans. A bird fluttered from a branch above them, sending a spray of droplets onto the path.

About thirty yards in, the cry came again. Louder this time. Clearer.

Definitely a foal.

A very young one.

Riley looked at Emma, all color draining from her face. "That is not possible. No one turns their horses out here."

Emma did not answer. She just hurried forward.

They followed the sound until the trail dipped sharply toward the old logging path. Fallen branches tangled across the ground from the last storm. Emma climbed over them carefully, using a trunk for balance. Riley steadied the flashlight and guided her footing.

Then Emma saw movement through the brambles. Something small shifted behind the branches.

Her breath caught.

A foal.

Barely old enough to stand steady.

Thin. Mud-smeared. Trembling.

Its small sides rose and fell rapidly with frightened breaths.

The foal was tangled in a cluster of long branches, its front leg stuck beneath a fallen limb. It cried weakly again, the sound trailing off into a soft, hoarse whimper.

Emma felt her chest tighten. She dropped to her knees and slowly approached the little horse. "It is all right. It is all right. We will help you."

Riley crouched beside her. "Be careful. It might panic."

But the foal did not try to run. It just stared at Emma with wide, glassy eyes, as if too tired to fight or flee. Emma reached out and stroked the mud-cold coat gently. The foal flinched but did not pull away.

"We need to free him," Emma whispered.

Riley nodded and held the branches aside while Emma lifted the limb trapping the foal's leg. It took both of them shifting their weight carefully to roll it aside. The foal stumbled forward, nearly collapsing, and Emma wrapped her arms around its neck to steady it. It smelled like wet leaves and fear and something else she could not quite name.

"It is all right," she whispered again. "You are safe now."

Riley tapped her phone awake. "I am calling Dale."

But before she could dial, the sound of hooves clattered behind them. They turned to see Dale approaching on horseback with Willow in tow. He must have noticed the mare's panic and followed their tracks. His face was tight with concern.

"What did you girls find?" he called, dismounting.

Riley pointed. "A foal. Just wandering out here."

Dale's eyes widened. He knelt beside the small horse, running experienced hands over its sides. "Well now, this is not good. This little one should not be here. Not at all."

He looked at Emma. "You two did the right thing. Let's get it to the barn."

Together, they guided the foal up the trail. Willow walked softly beside them, head lowered, ears tilted toward the frightened baby. She made a soft, deep sound in her throat every few steps, a comforting sound Emma had never heard from her before.

The foal leaned into Emma the whole way. Each time she removed her hand, it wobbled sideways as if searching for her again. She could feel the small heartbeat fluttering like a scared bird beneath its skin.

Back at the barn, everything shifted into quick action. Dale phoned the vet. Emma and Riley prepared a small stall with fresh blankets and warm water. Mia arrived rubbing sleep from her eyes and gasped when she saw the foal.

"Where did it come from?" she asked.

Emma shook her head. "We do not know."

The foal sank into the straw with a tired huff. Emma stayed by its side, brushing out leaves and bits of twig tangled in its coat. Its eyes drifted closed, but each time Emma moved, the foal twitched nervously.

"You can stay with it," Dale said softly. "Sometimes being close helps more than medicine."

Riley stood on the other side of the stall, arms folded. But her usual sharpness had softened. "It likes you," she said quietly. "That is weird."

Emma smiled faintly. "He just needs someone."

"Maybe," Riley said. "Or maybe you smell like apples."

Emma laughed for the first time that morning.

But her smile faded when she noticed Willow pacing slightly in her stall again. The mare's ears flicked toward the woods, toward the direction of the old path. A restless, unsettled movement rippled through Willow's muscles.

Emma followed Willow's gaze. The woods behind the barn were still. The fog lingered low over the grass. Nothing moved.

Yet the feeling from earlier returned.

That prickling sense that something was not right.

A soft crunch echoed from the far side of the paddock fence. Not loud enough to be a person walking. Not light enough to be a rabbit. Something in between. Something deliberate.

Emma turned, but the only thing she saw was the line of pines and the faint trail that led deeper into the forest. She stared for a long moment, waiting for another sound.

Nothing.

Just silence and morning light.

Then, from the barn entrance, Mia spoke again. "Did you hear that?"

Emma swallowed. "Hear what?"

"I thought I heard something moving out there," Mia said. "Maybe it was nothing."

Riley shrugged. "It was probably a deer."

But Emma felt the hairs on her arms rise.

She glanced at the foal curled into the straw.

She looked at Willow, still staring toward the woods.

She listened to the faint wind brushing the grass.

The ranch was supposed to feel safe.

It had always felt safe.

Yet this morning, it felt as if the woods were watching.

Waiting.

Holding a secret deep within the trees.

Emma pressed her palm gently to the foal's trembling neck.

"Whatever happened," she whispered, "you are safe with us now."

But inside, she wondered if safety was something she could truly promise.

Because the woods did not feel empty.

Not anymore.

Chapter Two

The foal slept in fits, stirring every few minutes as if unsure whether it was allowed to rest. Each time it twitched or whimpered, Emma felt herself tense, worried that the fragile breathing might change or fade. She stayed close, leaning against the stall wall, her legs pulled to her chest and her hands wrapped around her knees. The straw crackled softly beneath her as she shifted now and then to give the young horse space, though it always seemed to drift toward her again, nudging its nose against her boot or shoulder. Dawn light filtered through the barn windows in thin golden slants that brightened as the sun climbed, lending the air a warm shimmer that made the dust motes dance like pale sparks.

Riley stood outside the stall leaning against the wooden rail, arms crossed, watching with a mixture of curiosity, stubbornness, and something quieter that Emma recognized only because she was beginning to understand Riley's layers. Riley hated looking worried. She hated looking soft. But her eyes kept drifting back to the foal as if trying to solve a puzzle she did not want to admit she cared about. Mia sat on an overturned bucket nearby, combing tangles out of her own hair while she shot occasional sympathetic looks toward the baby horse.

The barn felt strangely hushed. Even the older geldings who usually stomped and snorted during feeding time seemed to keep to themselves, their movements gentle and restrained as if they understood that a frightened newcomer needed peace. Willow had stopped pacing, though her posture remained alert, muscles taut beneath her chestnut coat whenever she glanced toward the woods beyond the paddock. Emma noticed that Willow's ears kept angling forward at the slightest unusual sound. It reminded Emma of how her own heart had jumped at every rustle earlier.

When Dale returned to the barn leading the vet, Dr. Huxley, the atmosphere shifted again. The vet was a wiry man with silvering hair and kind eyes that could soften a nervous animal without needing to say a word. He carried a worn leather bag and crouched beside the little foal with a practiced gentleness that made Emma feel slightly reassured. The foal flinched at first, but Emma whispered soothing words and laid her hand on its back, and it soon went still under her touch.

Dr. Huxley examined the foal with serious concentration, running his hands along its legs, checking its eyes, mouth, and heartbeat, then gently coaxing it to stand so he could assess the range of movement. Emma noticed how thin the foal was, how its ribs pressed faintly against its coat. It seemed exhausted from its ordeal, but as it stood unsteadily, it leaned instinctively into Emma again as if she were a lifeline. She felt the fragile warmth of its body through her jeans and held her breath, willing it to stay strong.

Riley leaned over the stall door, trying to sound casual even though worry softened her voice. "Is something wrong with it?" she asked.

Dr. Huxley shook his head slowly. "Not wrong exactly," he said. "Just weak. Mild dehydration. Some scrapes and scratches from the branches. Nothing broken. But it is far too young to be out there on its own. Someone would have had to abandon it, or something drove its mother away."

Mia blinked with disbelief. "Why would anyone abandon a foal? That is like leaving a puppy in the middle of nowhere."

The vet sighed quietly. "There are many kinds of people in the world, Mia. Not all of them make kind decisions." He reached into his bag and pulled out a small device, running it along the foal's neck. A faint beep sounded but no information appeared on the scanner's small screen. "No microchip," he said. "Which is unusual for a young horse in this area. Most breeders chip foals soon after birth."

Emma's chest tightened. The thought of anyone being careless or cruel enough to leave a baby horse alone in the woods made her stomach twist. "Could it have wandered from a nearby ranch?" she asked, wanting to believe a safer explanation.

Dr. Huxley shook his head. "Not likely this far in. Foals do not go on long adventures. They stick close to their mothers, and their mothers stick even closer. And the woods are thick. No one would turn their horses loose near here. Too many risks. Too little grazing."

Riley stepped inside the stall, kneeling a few feet from the foal. It startled slightly, but Emma stroked its neck again, reminding it that the barn was safe. Riley's face softened as she reached out and gently patted its side. "Where did you come from?" she murmured.

The foal blinked up at her with wide, liquid eyes. It was small, likely only a few weeks old. Its coat was a pale reddish brown, lighter than Willow's, its mane nothing more than a wispy fringe. There was a small white marking on its forehead shaped like a crooked star. When the light hit it, the marking looked almost as if someone had brushed a stroke of paint there.

Dale stood behind the girls with one hand on the stall door. "Someone must have dumped it," he said quietly. "Which makes me angry. I do not know who would do such a thing, but this little one could not have gotten far with that leg caught in the branches."

Emma swallowed that thought. She had seen enough worry from the adults to know they were already thinking along the same lines.

The foal had not simply strayed from a pasture. Something more unsettling was at play.

"Will it be okay?" Emma asked.

"With care and rest," Dr. Huxley replied. "It needs warmth, fluids, and food in small amounts for a while. And it needs calm. Which means no running about and no overcrowding its stall." His eyes flicked to Mia, who blushed and scooted farther back on the bucket.

Emma let out a breath she had been holding. "I can help," she said. "I can stay with him. Or her. I guess we do not even know which."

"It is a colt," Dr. Huxley said with a small smile. "And it seems he has already decided you are his person. Sometimes animals choose faster than humans expect." He stood and dusted straw from his knees. "I will come back this afternoon to check on him again. Make sure he has plenty of water and a bit of mash. Not too much at once. His stomach is still delicate."

Dale nodded. "We will take care of him." He glanced at Emma and Riley. "But no more wandering into the woods without telling someone. That could have been dangerous."

Emma's cheeks warmed. She knew he was right. They should have asked for help first. But if they had gone all the way back to the barn for an adult, the foal might have struggled longer, or gotten hurt worse. Still, the concern in Dale's voice made her promise herself she would be more careful next time.

After the vet left, Emma and Riley settled on either side of the small colt. Mia went to fetch warm water and a small container of mash, careful not to overfill it. The colt lifted his head, sniffed weakly, and began to eat with tentative bites that soon grew more eager. Watching him brought a thick kind of relief to Emma's chest, though she could not explain why she felt so protective already. Maybe it was because she recognized the same lonely, uncertain expression she had once worn when she arrived at Saddle Creek. She knew what it felt like to be lost.

As the colt ate, Emma noticed a small scrape on the underside of his jaw and reached out to dab it with a damp cloth Riley handed her. The colt jerked slightly, but Riley steadied him, her hand gentle near his shoulder. Emma found herself smiling at Riley. She had expected Riley to tease her for being sappy over a foal, but Riley looked fully focused, as if she too wanted to make the colt feel safe.

"I think he likes you too," Emma said.

Riley shrugged, though a faint smile tugged at one corner of her mouth. "Maybe he likes anyone who is not a tree branch trapping his leg."

Emma laughed, but then her mind drifted back to the woods, and her smile faded. The memory of that faint cry echoing through the trees lingered in her head, along with the rustling she had heard after dawn. "Do you think someone left him there on purpose?" she asked quietly.

Riley hesitated. "I do not know. But I do not like how close he was to the old logging path. No one goes there anymore. Not unless they are trying to avoid being seen."

Emma thought about the fresh bootprint she had noticed earlier. She had not mentioned it yet, partly because she was not completely sure what she had seen, and partly because the thought of someone lurking near the woods made her uncomfortable. She debated telling Riley but decided to wait until she understood it better herself. Maybe she had imagined it. Maybe the ground had been uneven and her eyes had played tricks on her.

Mia returned with the mash and placed it gently in front of the foal. "Does he have a name?" she asked, brushing a stray piece of straw from her sleeve.

Emma glanced at the colt's crooked star marking. "Maybe something that fits his little star," she said. "But I think we should wait before naming him. Dale always says not to name animals too soon. It makes it harder if they belong to someone else."

Riley leaned her arms on the stall door again. "I doubt anyone is coming to claim him," she said. "If they wanted him, they would have taken care of him."

Emma did not respond. She did not want to believe anyone could abandon a foal, but the possibility had settled heavily in her thoughts.

As the morning stretched on, the barn grew busier with the usual rhythms of feeding, grooming, and preparing horses for the day. Emma spent most of the time near the colt, helping him drink small sips and brushing dirt gently off his coat. Riley came and went, checking on Storm and helping Dale with chores, but she always paused by the colt's stall before leaving again, her expression lingering with quiet concern.

Mia went to fetch fresh blankets and returned carrying a colorful one with a faded pattern of horses printed on it. "I had this when I was younger," she said shyly. "It used to be in my room. But maybe he can use it now."

Emma spread it across the straw, creating a soft corner where the colt curled up again, tucking his legs close to his body. Emma sat beside him, letting her hand rest lightly on his back. The colt's breathing steadied under her touch, and she felt a sense of calm she had not realized she needed.

But even as she watched the colt drift to sleep, Emma felt that same prickling sensation she had sensed earlier. Willow's restless glances toward the woods, the faint noise she had heard, the strange hush over the ranch. Something about the morning felt unfinished, like a story beginning in shadows.

Dale returned around mid-morning carrying a bucket of warm water and a roll of fresh bandaging. He knelt beside the colt again, lifting one of its hooves carefully. "No signs of infection," he said. "That is good. He is stronger than he looks."

Emma brushed her hand over the colt's head, smoothing the short wisps of mane. "Do you think he came from far away?"

"Hard to tell," Dale replied. "But there are a few ranches across the ridge. Most keep their foals well guarded. I will make some calls later to see if anyone is missing a colt." He paused, then added in a tone that confirmed his suspicion. "But I doubt we will get a call back."

Emma felt her stomach twist. "Why would someone want to get rid of a foal?"

Dale glanced at her thoughtfully. "Some people care too much about money. Too little about life. A foal that does not meet their standards becomes a burden. It is a terrible truth, but it happens."

Emma looked down at the small colt who had curled against her once more. She could not imagine anyone seeing him as anything other than precious.

She thought of Willow again, of the way the mare had approached the colt gently, as if recognizing something Emma could not name. Willow had always been sensitive to subtle shifts in mood or environment, and her unease continued to weigh on Emma's thoughts.

When noon approached, the sun cast a warm glow across the barn aisles. The foal slept more soundly now, his breathing steady. Emma stretched her legs and stood, brushing straw from her hoodie. Riley returned from helping Dale with the hay storage and wiped her forehead with her sleeve.

"You stayed with him all morning," Riley said, trying to sound casual but failing to hide her admiration.

Emma shrugged with a small smile. "He needed company."

Riley nodded and leaned her elbows on the stall door again. "You have that effect. Animals feel safe with you."

Emma felt warmth at Riley's words. They were not easy compliments, the kind Riley offered without thinking. Most of the time Riley guarded her thoughts like they were something fragile. When she did lower her guard, the kindness always surprised Emma in a way that made her chest feel full.

Mia approached them carrying two water bottles and passed one to Emma. "I think Dale wants us to take a break," she said. "He told me to tell you that you cannot take care of a foal if you pass out from hunger."

Emma realized she had barely eaten since the banana early that morning. She stepped outside with the girls, the sunlight bright and warm on her face. They sat on the fence rail overlooking the paddocks, sipping water while the horses grazed quietly below.

The ranch looked peaceful. Birds fluttered between the fence posts. A light breeze rustled the tall grass. In the distance, a figure led a horse along a distant trail, too far away for Emma to make out who it was. She saw the glint of a bridle and the pale flash of sunlight on a white shirt. The rider moved steadily toward the ridge, disappearing behind a cluster of tall pines at the edge of Saddle Creek's property.

Emma watched until they vanished, a brief moment that seemed unimportant yet caught her attention for reasons she could not explain. Perhaps it was just the way the figure had paused at one point to look behind them before continuing up the path, or perhaps it was because Emma felt so attuned to every tiny shift around the ranch that morning. Either way, the thought lingered in her mind.

Riley followed her gaze. "Someone from the trails?"

"I think so," Emma replied. "I have not seen that horse before though."

Riley squinted at the ridge. "There are a few riders who pass through. Could be someone new." She paused, frowning slightly. "Or someone lost."

Emma looked again, but the trail was empty now. "Maybe," she said. But the feeling stuck with her. First the bootprint she thought she had seen. Then the rustling before dawn. Now a stranger riding near the northern ridge. None of it felt connected, but each piece left a tiny mark on her mind like stepping stones she had not wanted to notice.

After resting for a bit, the girls returned to the barn. The colt stirred awake, lifted his head, and gave a small soft whinny when Emma approached. She laughed quietly and knelt beside him again, brushing his neck with gentle strokes.

"You are safe," she whispered. "You are not alone anymore."

The colt leaned against her again, warm and trusting. Emma felt his heartbeat beneath her hand and realized how quickly she had bonded with him. She knew she should not get attached, but her heart had already stepped across that line without asking permission.

Riley stepped into the stall again, her expression unreadable as she watched Emma and the colt. She sat down on the straw beside them, brushing her hand lightly across the colt's side.

"He really does like you," Riley said.

Emma smiled. "He will like you too once he knows you better."

Riley shrugged without looking up. "Maybe."

They stayed there in quiet companionship while afternoon rolled slowly over Saddle Creek. Horses shifted and nickered, sunlight warmed the wooden beams overhead, and dust motes floated lazily in the golden haze. The colt began to drift back to sleep again, his small breaths steady and warm.

Dale checked on them and nodded approvingly at the progress. "You girls have done a good job. Keep helping him drink, and let him sleep. He needs rest more than anything."

Emma nodded. "We will take care of him."

Riley nodded as well, though she added quickly, "But we probably should not get too attached."

Mia leaned against the stall door with a grin. "Says the girl who has been here almost as long as Emma."

Riley flushed slightly and flicked a piece of straw at Mia. "I am allowed to care without making a big deal about it."

Emma laughed quietly. She knew better than to tease Riley too much. Riley cared deeply, maybe more deeply than most people, and it showed in the way she returned to check on the colt no matter how often she tried to act indifferent.

The rest of the afternoon unfolded in a warm, slow rhythm. They tended to the horses, cleaned the tack room, swept the aisles, and helped Dale unload a delivery of feed. The work was familiar, grounding, and steady. But every few minutes Emma's eyes drifted toward the woods, searching for movement that never came.

By early evening, the ranch settled into its usual end-of-day calm.

The Lost Foal Mystery (Young adult horse fiction)

The sun cast long shadows across the paddocks, turning the grass a soft amber. Birds quieted their calls. Horses shifted in their stalls, preparing for the night. Emma sat with the colt one last time, brushing his coat with slow, soothing strokes. He was stronger already, his eyes brighter and his breathing steadier.

"You are going to be okay," she whispered.

Riley lingered in the doorway. "We should head home soon."

Emma nodded reluctantly. She stood, brushed her jeans off, and gave the colt one final pat. "Sleep well," she murmured.

As they walked out of the barn, Emma turned to look toward the ridge again. The trail entrance was shadowy and still. No riders. No strangers. No rustling in the leaves.

But Willow lifted her head suddenly from her stall and stared in the same direction, ears pricked. Something glimmered faintly between the trees. A soft flicker, like light reflecting off metal or glass.

Emma froze.

Riley followed her gaze. "What is it?"

"I thought I saw something," Emma said quietly. "Something shiny."

Riley squinted at the trees. "Probably nothing."

But Willow stamped her hoof once, a sharp protest that echoed through the barn.

Emma felt the prickle again along her arms, that same uneasy whisper she had felt at dawn.

Something had been out there this morning.

Something had watched from the woods.

The colt had not been lost.

He had been running from something.

Emma swallowed hard.

The story was only beginning.

Chapter Three

Morning sunlight filtered through the barn's open doors, stretching across the worn wooden floorboards in long, warm stripes. Dust particles drifted lazily through the beams of light, giving the air a quiet golden shimmer. The foal was already awake when Emma arrived, his small head lifted, his ears pricking forward when he recognized her footsteps. She felt a warmth expand in her chest as he struggled to his feet and took one wobbly step toward her.

He still moved unsteadily, but his eyes were brighter today, clearer, as if he had finally slept deeply enough to let his mind catch up with his body. Emma stepped inside the stall and rubbed his soft neck, letting him lean against her side. She felt his breath on her arm, warm and damp, and she smiled despite the lingering unease from the day before.

"Good morning," she whispered.

The foal pressed closer, his small tail flicking once. He had grown more comfortable with her quickly, far faster than some of the other rescue horses she had met at Saddle Creek. That made Emma wonder what kind of home he had come from. Horses with gentle pasts trusted easily. Horses with rough ones took time. But this colt acted like someone had once shown him kindness, which made the idea of being abandoned in the woods even harder to understand.

Riley appeared at the stall door a moment later, her hair in a braid and a smudge of hay clinging to her sleeve. She looked like she had been awake for hours already. Storm's feed bucket sat in her hand, yet she stood there instead of returning to her chores.

"He looks better," Riley said. Her voice sounded almost relieved, though she tried to hide it behind a casual shrug. "Stronger."

Emma nodded. "He slept a lot. But he was restless too. A couple times he woke up like something startled him."

Riley frowned. "Startled him how?"

"Like he felt something was near," Emma said. "He kept looking toward the barn door."

Riley hesitated before stepping fully into the stall. She crouched beside the colt, checking his legs and sides with light touches. "You know that could just be nerves. He had a rough day."

Emma knew Riley was right. Animals often reacted to their memories before their surroundings. But something felt off. A lingering feeling from yesterday's rustling in the trees. A sense that they had been watched.

Before Riley could say more, Mia burst through the barn doors carrying a folded newspaper. She waved it in the air with wide eyes.

"You girls need to see this," Mia said, breathless. "There is a story about some breeders over in Pine Hollow. They had an inspection last month. It says a couple of their animals were missing. They could not account for them."

Riley stood. "Missing?"

Mia nodded as she flipped the newspaper open. "It says one mare was found wandering down a back road. And two foals were just gone. Like vanished. The report says the owners claimed someone stole them."

Emma felt a chill crawl slowly up her spine. "Do you think our foal was one of them?"

Riley took the paper, scanning the article. "Pine Hollow is far. But not impossible. Someone could have transported them. But stealing foals?" She narrowed her eyes. "That does not make sense."

"It does if the breeder wanted to hide something," Mia said. "Like, if the foals were sick or weak."

Emma reached for the paper. She skimmed the lines quickly, her heart beating harder with every paragraph. The article talked about complaints from neighbors, whispers about shady practices, and rumors that the ranch owners cared more about money than the welfare of their horses. It mentioned foals taken away before they were fully weaned. It mentioned animals being shuffled around to avoid inspections.

The foal nudged Emma's hand, as if seeking reassurance.

"I do not like this," Emma said softly.

Riley's expression tightened. "We need to tell Dale."

"We should wait for the vet first," Mia said. "He might know more."

"He cannot if we do not show him," Riley argued. She folded the newspaper. "We are taking this to him."

Emma followed Riley as she strode across the barn to Dale, who was sorting through tack in the gear room. He looked up when they approached, wiping his hands on a rag. Riley presented the paper and launched straight into an explanation.

Dale listened, his brow furrowing deeper with each detail. When he finished reading, he set the newspaper on the counter and sighed heavily.

"I know the place mentioned in this article," he said. "I have heard rumors for years that they cut corners. But this is the first I've heard of animals going missing."

Emma looked back toward the foal's stall. "He was near the old logging path. If someone wanted to get rid of him quietly, that would be a place to do it."

Dale rubbed his chin. "It is possible, but not certain. That ridge trail is used by hunters sometimes, and by the forestry service workers. A loose horse could have traveled there."

Riley folded her arms. "A foal this small would not go far without its mother."

"That is true," Dale said. "But we need facts, not guesses. The vet will be here soon. Let us see what he thinks."

Emma nodded, though worry still clung to her thoughts. As they walked back toward the foal, she caught sight of movement outside the barn. A figure walking near the fence line. The sunlight hid most of the details, but she saw the shape of someone tall, wearing a dark jacket, pausing by the trail that led toward the northern woods.

Emma slowed. The person stood still for an odd moment, as if watching something, then turned and walked away.

Riley glanced over her shoulder. "Who was that?"

"I do not know," Emma said. "Did you recognize them?"

Riley shook her head. "Probably a hiker. Or a random trail rider."

Emma wanted to believe that. She really did. But the figure had seemed too still, too deliberate, too aware.

Before she could say more, Dr. Huxley arrived again. His truck rumbled into the driveway, and the engine shut off with a soft sputter. He walked into the barn carrying his bag, smiling briefly when he saw the colt already standing.

"Well now," he said, kneeling beside the foal, "you look brighter than yesterday. That is a good sign."

Emma watched closely as Dr. Huxley ran through another examination. He checked the colt's heartbeat, his temperature, and his joints. Then he removed a small flashlight and gently pried open the colt's mouth, checking for abnormalities. After a long moment of silent inspection, he eased back on his heels.

"What is it?" Emma asked, noticing the faint crease between his brows.

Dr. Huxley rested a hand on the colt's neck. "This fellow has a slightly crooked jaw. It is mild, but it is a congenital condition. Means he was born with it."

"Is it serious?" Emma asked quickly.

"Not life-threatening," the vet said. "Many horses with slight jaw misalignment live full lives. But it affects show value. Some breeders consider it a flaw."

Riley let out a dry laugh. "So someone might have abandoned him because he was not perfect."

Dr. Huxley gave a slow, sad nod. "Unfortunately, yes. That happens more than I like to admit."

Emma felt her chest tighten. "We found an article about a place where animals went missing," she said. "We thought maybe he came from there."

The vet blinked. "Let me see."

Riley handed him the folded newspaper. He read silently, his lips pressing into a thin line.

"I visited this ranch once," Dr. Huxley said after a long moment. "They had a strict breeding program. Very strict. If a foal did not meet expectations, they would sell it quickly or move it to another facility. But I did not see anything that looked like abuse." He paused. "Still, reports like this do not come from nowhere."

Emma felt the foal nuzzle her sleeve again, pressing closer as if sensing her rising worry. She laid her hand on his back and whispered a quiet reassurance.

Dr. Huxley returned the newspaper. "It is possible your colt came from that ranch. But we need more information. I will make some calls."

He rose to leave but paused at the barn door. "Dale," he said, "keep an eye on your fences. If someone abandoned this foal, they may return to look around."

Emma felt the hairs on her arms lift again. Dale nodded grimly as the vet departed.

Riley turned to Emma, lowering her voice. "This is getting weird."

Emma nodded. "I keep thinking about the woods."

"What about them?" Mia asked, appearing at Riley's elbow.

Emma hesitated. "Yesterday morning, before we found the colt, I heard something. Something like a person moving. And I think I saw a bootprint. Fresh."

Riley whirled toward her. "Why did you not say anything?"

"I was not sure," Emma said, feeling heat rise in her cheeks. "I thought maybe I imagined it."

"You did not imagine it," Riley insisted. "Storm was restless too. And Willow kept pacing. Something was there."

Mia crossed her arms tightly. "Maybe it was just a hunter."

"Maybe," Emma said. But her voice lacked confidence.

The three girls stood in silence for a moment, the barn suddenly feeling bigger and more hollow around them.

Riley stepped into the colt's stall again and crouched beside him. "Can we name him now? I feel weird calling him the colt."

Emma laughed softly despite the tension. "What about Rusty?"

Mia nodded eagerly. "Rusty is cute."

Riley touched the colt's forehead gently. "Rusty," she repeated. "Yeah. That fits."

Emma felt warmth bloom in her chest again. "Then Rusty it is."

Rusty lifted his head, as if approving the choice.

They spent the rest of the morning tending to Rusty, helping him drink and brushing his coat carefully. As they worked, the barn's usual noises returned. Horses nickered. Birds sang outside. Dale moved through the aisles with the steady rhythm of chores. On the surface, everything seemed normal.

But underneath, Emma felt something shifting.

At lunch, she stepped outside to sit on the fence rail, letting the breeze cool her face. Riley and Mia sat beside her, each of them quiet for a long moment. The paddocks spread out before them, the grass bright under the midday sun. But Emma's eyes drifted toward the trail leading into the woods.

A faint glimmer caught her eye. Something metallic in the dirt. She slid off the fence and walked slowly toward it. Riley and Mia followed without question.

Emma crouched and picked up a small piece of metal half buried in the soil. It was a narrow bolt, the kind used on trailers or equipment. But this one had a strange scratch on it, as if someone had tried to scrape off a marking.

Riley took it from her hand and inspected it. "This did not fall off Dale's equipment. His stuff is all new. And clean."

Mia lowered her voice. "So someone else was here."

Emma stared at the trees. The woods felt deeper suddenly, darker even in full daylight.

"Someone was here," Emma whispered. "Something scared Rusty's mother away. Something made him run."

Riley's jaw tightened. "We need to figure out who. And why they left him."

Emma nodded. She felt Rusty's trust like a weight on her shoulders, something fragile and important.

The colt had no past.

But someone out there knew his story.

And Emma was determined to find out who.

Chapter Four

Morning drifted into afternoon at Saddle Creek with a warmth that made the fields shimmer in soft waves. Birds chattered from the fence posts, and somewhere near the hay shed, goats bleated in their strange, broken cries that always made Emma smile. The ranch usually felt steady and familiar by this time of day, but today there was something sharper beneath the surface, as if a string had been pulled too tight. Emma felt it in her chest each time she glanced toward Rusty's stall, and she felt it again whenever she noticed Riley's shoulders tense at the mention of chores involving the foal.

It started small, almost invisible. Riley snapped at Storm when he nudged her too insistently for attention, and she turned away when Emma asked if she wanted help with grooming. These were the kinds of things Riley did when she was bothered by something but did not want to admit it. Normally Emma would have found a way to tease a smile out of her, but today her own worries swirled too close to the surface for easy distraction.

The events of the last two days weighed heavily in her thoughts. Something had brought Rusty to the woods, and every instinct whispered that it had not been an accident. The bolt she had found near the paddock still sat in her pocket, cool and heavy, a reminder that the ranch was not as isolated as it felt. Whoever had been in the woods might come back, and the thought of Rusty's fragile body trembling alone in the darkness made Emma's stomach twist.

She spent the first part of the morning tending to Rusty with gentle patience. The colt responded to her touch each time with the same trustful leaning, his eyes closing halfway while she brushed him with slow, even strokes. He was growing stronger, though he still tired quickly and sometimes startled at shadows or sudden noises. She tried to soothe him, whispering quiet words and scratching behind his ears until he relaxed. Riley had helped earlier, but each time she came into the stall she seemed distracted, her mind drifting elsewhere.

Emma decided not to push it. They had both had a stressful morning. But by the time lunch arrived, the tension between them had grown thick enough that even Mia noticed.

"You two are being weird," Mia said as she tucked her hair behind her ears. She spoke lightly, but her brow furrowed. "Did something happen?"

Emma shook her head. "Nothing happened. Riley is just tired."

Riley snorted but said nothing. She kept her gaze on the hay she was tossing into Storm's trough, her movements sharper than usual. When she turned back, her cheeks were flushed, and her eyes flicked toward Emma before she looked away again.

Mia glanced between them. "Okay, well never mind then." She grabbed her water bottle and started toward the tack room. "I will be in the saddle soap section if anyone wants to talk like normal humans."

Emma tried to smile, but her chest ached with the knowledge that something was coming, something she could feel building in every stiff silence. She wanted to ask Riley directly what was wrong, but the moment she opened her mouth, Riley walked past her and headed toward the paddock with Storm.

Fine, Emma thought. If Riley wanted space, she could have it. She was not going to force a conversation Riley did not want.

Still, the quiet felt heavy.

Dale's voice rang out from near the barn entrance. "Emma, Mia, Riley. I need help reorganizing the feed room. And after that I want the three of you to check fence line seven. There was a tree fall last night, and I want to make sure nothing broke."

Emma's heart skipped a beat. Fence line seven was near the woods. Near the place where Rusty had been found. She swallowed and nodded. Riley hesitated but ultimately headed toward the feed room without complaint.

The work was simple at first. They piled feed bags, stacked buckets, swept the dusty floor, and sorted the grooming supplies into neat rows. The smell of oats and molasses filled the air, earthy and sweet. Usually chores like this gave Emma a sense of peace. Today they only reminded her of how awkward the silence between her and Riley had become.

Emma lifted a bag of grain and felt Riley watching her. When she turned, Riley quickly looked away. But it was enough to make Emma speak.

"Are you still upset with me?" Emma asked quietly.

Riley paused, her hands still on the stack of tools she was arranging. Her jaw tightened. "I am not upset."

"You look upset."

"I said I am not."

Emma exhaled slowly. "Okay."

Riley sighed. "It is just a lot, okay? All of this. Finding Rusty. Not knowing where he came from. Dale being on edge. You acting like you need to protect the whole ranch."

"I am not acting like that," Emma said. But even to her own ears, the words sounded defensive.

Riley shook her head, her braid swishing behind her. "You do not see it. Whenever something happens, you rush into it like it is your responsibility."

Emma set down the bag of grain with more force than she intended. "We found a foal alone in the woods. Of course I care."

"And I do not?" Riley snapped.

Emma flinched. "I did not say that."

"You did not have to," Riley muttered. She brushed past Emma to grab another feed bucket.

Emma stood still for a moment, feeling the words sting deeper than she expected. Riley had always been competitive, prickly, tough around the edges, but she had never been unfair. Or at least, Emma did not think she had. Today though, Riley's defensiveness seemed to stem from something more fragile than pride. Something Emma did not understand yet.

"We are supposed to be a team," Emma said softly. "You and me."

Riley paused, her shoulders lifting with a long breath. For a moment Emma thought she might turn and confess what was weighing on her. Instead Riley said, "Teams work when both people try. Not when one person decides everything alone."

Emma's chest tightened. "Riley, I am not deciding anything alone."

"You told Dale about the bolt without me. You talked to the vet about the article before I even knew what you were thinking. You found that bootprint thing and did not mention it for a whole day."

"You barely wanted to talk," Emma said. "I did not want to bother you."

"You bother me more when you do stuff and do not tell me," Riley said. "I care about Rusty too."

Emma's throat thickened. She wanted to say that she knew Riley cared. That she had seen it in the way Riley checked Rusty's stall whenever she thought no one was looking. But the words tangled inside her.

"Then say something," Emma whispered. "If something is wrong, just say so."

Riley looked at her for a long moment. Her blue eyes were full of something raw, something Emma did not entirely recognize. But instead of answering, Riley looked away.

"We should finish the feed room," she said quietly.

Emma wanted to argue, but the tone in Riley's voice made her stop. It was not anger. It was fear. A fear of something deeper than Rusty or the woods.

Or maybe, Emma realized with a sharp ache, it was fear of losing the bond they had begun to form.

They finished the chore in silence. Mia returned with a newly scrubbed bridle and looked between them with wide, questioning eyes.

"Are you two okay?" she asked.

"Fine," Riley said without looking up.

Emma forced a smile. "Just tired."

Mia raised a skeptical eyebrow but said nothing.

After they finished in the feed room, the three girls headed out toward fence line seven with gloves and a small toolkit. The sky had shifted into a soft overcast, turning the fields a muted green. The air smelled faintly of rain, though no clouds looked dark enough to release any.

Fence line seven stretched along the edge of the woods where the trees grew thick and tall. The path Dale used for checking the fence curved along the forest's edge like a thin scar separating cultivated land from untamed wildness. Emma's stomach tightened as they approached.

Mia spoke first. "It looks peaceful."

Emma nodded but did not trust the stillness. The woods were quiet in a way that felt almost deliberate. As if the trees themselves were waiting.

They found the fallen branch quickly. It had collapsed over the top rail of the fence, bending the wood downward but not breaking it fully. Riley and Emma lifted it carefully while Mia held the fence steady. Together they worked in a steady rhythm, clearing the heavy branch bit by bit.

Emma glanced into the woods as they worked, scanning the shadows for movement. Every shifting branch made her heartbeat jump a little. She tried not to let her imagination run wild, but after everything that had happened, caution felt necessary.

When the branch was cleared, Riley inspected the fence posts. "Looks like the wire is bent," she said. "We need to tighten it."

Mia found the replacement clips in the toolkit and offered them to Riley. They began working on the repair while Emma checked more of the ground near the fence. That was when she saw it.

A hoofprint. Fresh. Not from a full-grown horse, but larger than Rusty's tiny tracks. The shape was clear in the damp soil. Someone had come through here recently.

"Riley," Emma whispered. "Look."

Riley joined her. Her breath hitched quietly. "That is not Storm's. And it is not Willow's hoof size."

Mia crouched beside them. "That looks new."

Emma's mind raced. "Someone brought a horse through here."

"But why?" Riley asked. "No one rides on this side of the woods. The trails are on the opposite end."

Emma stepped closer to the fence. The woods loomed behind it, dark even in the soft daylight. She stared into the shadows, unable to shake the feeling that someone had stood in that exact spot recently.

"We need to tell Dale," Emma said.

Riley hesitated. "Should we tell him everything? Or wait?"

Emma looked at her sharply. "Of course we should tell him. This is important."

Riley's shoulders tensed. "I know that. I just mean maybe we should think first. Put all the pieces together."

Emma shook her head. "That is not our job. If something is happening on the ranch, Dale needs to know."

Riley looked frustrated again, the same look she had worn in the feed room. "You always rush."

"And you always hesitate," Emma said, before she could stop herself.

Riley blinked as if the words stung. Emma's chest tightened instantly with regret.

"I did not mean it like that," Emma said quickly. "I just meant we have to stay safe."

Riley looked down at her gloves, twisting the leather between her fingers. "I am trying to help too, Emma."

Emma stepped closer. "I know. I am sorry."

The apology hung in the air until Riley finally nodded. "We will tell Dale together."

Emma felt her shoulders relax slightly. The tension did not disappear, but it eased enough for them to continue working.

They finished repairing the fence, wiping sweat from their brows. The hoofprint still sat in the soil like a warning. When they returned to the barn, they found Dale fixing a hinge on one of the stall doors. Emma approached him first, the hoofprint still vivid in her thoughts.

"Dale," she said, "we found something near the fence."

His expression shifted instantly to concern. "What did you find?"

Emma explained about the hoofprint, the fresh soil, and the way it looked like someone had ridden through the woods. Riley added details about the fence and the direction the track faced. Dale listened quietly, his

face growing more serious with each word.

"Show me," he said.

They led him back to the fence line. He crouched near the hoofprint and studied it carefully.

"You girls were right to come get me," he said. "This is not from any of our horses."

Mia chewed her bottom lip. "Do you think it is connected to Rusty?"

Dale did not answer immediately. He stood slowly, scanning the woods. "I do not know. But I do not like it."

Emma glanced at Riley. Riley looked back, and their eyes met with shared worry. Whatever distance had formed earlier seemed less important now. Something was happening at Saddle Creek. Something none of them understood yet.

Dale walked the fence line, studying the trees, the soil, and the brush. After several minutes he turned back to them.

"I want the three of you to stay close to the barn for a while," he said. "No wandering into the woods. No riding past the lower paddocks. Not until we know more."

Emma's heart thudded. "Do you think someone is coming onto the ranch?"

"Not necessarily," Dale said carefully. "But someone was here recently, and I want to take precautions."

Riley folded her arms tightly. "We can help. We can keep watch."

Dale shook his head gently. "I appreciate it. But this is adult work. Your job is to stay safe."

Emma nodded, though worry still lingered. She rubbed her thumb over the edges of her gloves, trying to think. If someone had brought a horse through the woods, what were they doing? Were they scouting the area? Looking for something? Hiding something?

She thought again of Rusty trembling in the brambles. Someone had left him there. Someone who cared so little for a foal that they abandoned him in the cold darkness. That was not the kind of person who would hesitate to return if they felt threatened or desperate.

Emma followed Dale back to the barn, her steps slow, her mind swirling with questions she could not answer. Riley walked beside her, silent but close enough that their shoulders brushed lightly every few steps.

Inside the barn, the warmth of the horses greeted them with familiar comfort. Willow lifted her head and whinnied softly when she saw Emma. Rusty stirred in his stall and gave a faint, excited nicker when he spotted them.

Emma paused in front of his stall, watching his bright eyes and gentle movements. She felt Riley stop beside her.

Riley spoke quietly. "Sorry about earlier."

Emma looked at her with a soft smile. "I was sorry too."

Riley returned the smile, small but real. "We are okay?"

Emma nodded. "We are okay."

Rusty nudged the stall gate, almost like he agreed.

They both laughed, the tension finally breaking.

But even as the air between them eased, Emma felt the weight of the hoofprint lingering in her thoughts. Rusty's past was beginning to pull shadows into their lives, shadows that reached beyond Saddle Creek, shadows that whispered of secrets still hidden in the woods.

The storm had not yet arrived.

But the wind had already changed.

And Emma sensed the first signs of a danger that would follow them long after the sun set.

Chapter Five

Morning sunlight broke through the clouds in soft, uneven patches as Emma, Riley, and Mia gathered near the barn entrance the next day. The air carried the fresh scent of dew and pine, mixed with the familiar warmth of hay. Horses shifted in their stalls, snorting softly, unaware of the tension swirling between the three girls. Ever since the hoofprint discovery, Dale had been stricter about staying close to the main yard, which made everything feel heavier, as if the ranch had become a woven basket with frayed edges.

Emma's eyes kept drifting toward Rusty's stall. The little colt had slept well and was growing steadier on his legs. He greeted her with a weak but bright nicker each morning, pushing his nose into her hand like he was checking to see if she was still real. His trust made her chest ache with something fierce and protective. She wanted to keep him safe, to make sure nothing frightened him again. But something about the woods still gnawed at her, a quiet whisper beneath her thoughts that refused to fade.

She brushed Rusty's soft coat while he nursed from the bottle Dale had prepared. Riley watched from the doorway, arms crossed loosely, her expression softer than the day before. Their argument still lingered in Emma's mind, not painfully, but like the last notes of a song that had finally ended. They had smoothed things over, but Emma could tell Riley was still sorting through her own feelings. She always did. Riley took longer to trust, longer to let things settle, but Emma knew the effort mattered.

Mia walked into the stall with a small bucket of warm mash. "He is eating better," she said, kneeling beside Rusty. "That is a good sign."

Emma nodded. "He is getting stronger." She hesitated. "Do you think he remembers what happened in the woods?"

Mia looked thoughtful. "Animals remember fear. But maybe he will forget it once he feels safe."

Emma hoped that was true. She rubbed Rusty's neck until he sighed softly. But when a loud clang echoed from outside, Rusty jumped, stumbling backward. His eyes widened, panicked for a moment. Emma knelt and cupped his face gently to calm him.

"It is all right," she whispered. "Nothing is going to hurt you."

Rusty's breathing slowed, but the tension in his small frame took longer to ease.

Riley stepped forward. "Something scared him in those woods," she said quietly. "Something that did not want him found."

Emma met her gaze, and they exchanged the same unspoken thought.

Whatever happened was not over yet.

After completing the morning chores, the three girls gathered near the tack room. Dale was busy repairing a gate hinge, and the ranch hands were stretched across the property tending to chores ahead of the weekend riding lessons. No one paid much attention to the girls except when Dale glanced up to make sure they stayed within sight.

"We are not supposed to go anywhere near the woods," Mia reminded them quietly.

Emma bit her lip. "I know. But I keep thinking about Rusty's tracks. And that hoofprint. If someone is coming through the woods, they might come back."

Riley lowered her voice. "We could check the lower trail. Just the edge. Not the deep woods. Dale would never know we left the fences."

Emma hesitated. She had promised herself to be more cautious. But the thought of unanswered questions gnawed at her. The hoofprint near the fence had not disappeared from her mind. Someone had brought a horse close to the ranch boundary recently. And that bolt she found days ago still felt significant, though she could not explain why.

"We go together," Emma said finally. "We look. We do not wander far. And if anything feels wrong, we come back immediately."

Riley nodded firmly. "Agreed."

Mia exhaled. "All right. But if Dale asks where we went, I am blaming both of you."

Emma smiled despite the tension. "Come on."

They slipped behind the paddocks and headed toward the lower trail entrance. The path was narrow but well worn, curving along the edge of the property. Birds trilled overhead, hopping from branch to branch, and sunlight flickered through the trees like scattered gold coins. From afar, the woods did not look threatening. But the closer they walked, the more the shadows thickened between the trunks, turning the trails into dark, twisting corridors.

Emma paused at the trail's edge. The air felt cooler here, as if the forest breathed on its own. She closed her eyes for a moment, listening. Only birds. Only wind. Yet beneath those familiar sounds, she sensed something else. A stillness too controlled, as if the woods watched them step closer.

They moved slowly, examining the ground on both sides of the trail. Mia pointed out a few hoofprints from recreational riders, but they were old and weathered. Riley bent down to study the soil, pressing her fingers into the dirt.

"Nothing fresh here," she said. "Not like yesterday."

Emma kept her gaze ahead. The trail curved toward an old logging road that had been abandoned years ago. Most riders avoided it because of the fallen brush and broken branches, but it was the direction Rusty had been found in. They reached the spot where the trail dipped into a slight valley. The ground here was softer, as if rainwater pooled there after storms.

Emma crouched. "Look."

Riley hurried to her side. A faint indentation marked the soil. Larger than Rusty's. Narrower than a full-size horse. Fresh enough to still hold its shape. Someone had been here recently.

"That is from a young horse," Riley whispered. "Not a foal. But not a fully grown one either."

Emma felt her heartbeat quicken. "Rusty was not alone."

Mia swallowed hard. "So he might have come with another horse."

Emma's breath caught. "Or he might have been led here by someone riding a young horse."

Riley stood slowly. "We should go back."

Emma shook her head. "Just a little farther."

Riley hesitated. "Emma."

"I want to see where this goes."

Mia shifted nervously. "We promised we would be careful."

Emma stepped forward. "We will be. I just need to know what happened."

Against their better judgment, the three continued along the trail until they reached the old logging clearing. Fallen trunks littered the ground, and tangled brush twisted across the path where nature had reclaimed what humans abandoned. Emma felt the air shift again. A faint smell hung there, like old smoke or sweat. Something recent. Something human.

"There," Riley said, pointing to a patch of flattened grass.

Emma approached carefully. Two sets of footprints stood visible. One set small, probably a younger rider or a teenager. The other larger. Adult. The marks crossed each other awkwardly, as if the two had stood facing one another.

"What were they doing here?" Mia asked.

Emma did not know. But something about the scene felt wrong. Her eyes scanned the clearing until she spotted something tiny glinting in a patch of sunlight.

She knelt and picked it up. "Another bolt."

Riley stared at it. "That is like the one you found outside Rusty's pen."

Emma nodded. "Someone has been replacing or tampering with equipment. Or dropping things."

Mia's voice trembled. "Should we leave?"

Before Emma could answer, a sharp crack echoed from deeper in the woods. A branch snapping. Heavy. Not like a deer or a squirrel. Something bigger.

Emma froze.

Riley grabbed her arm. "Go."

They stepped backward slowly, trying not to rustle the leaves. The woods remained silent for a long moment, but Emma sensed someone watching. The air thickened. Her pulse thundered in her ears.

Then another snap.

Closer.

"Run," Riley whispered.

The three girls bolted down the trail, dodging roots and branches. Emma heard the blood pounding in her chest, felt the breath burn her lungs. They did not look back until they reached the paddocks, panting and trembling. Dale had not noticed their absence yet. Horses grazed lazily as if nothing was wrong.

Mia collapsed onto the fence rail, clutching her side. "That was not an animal."

Riley nodded, wiping sweat from her forehead. "Someone was there."

Emma clutched both bolts tightly in her palm, her fingers shaking. "Someone wanted us gone."

Riley's eyes darkened. "And they almost got close enough to see us."

Emma took a slow, unsteady breath. "We need to tell Dale."

They walked quickly back to the barn. Dale noticed their pale faces the moment they stepped inside.

"What happened?" he asked.

Emma opened her palm, revealing both bolts. "We found more tracks."

"And someone is in the woods," Riley added. "Someone big. They followed us."

Dale stared at the bolts, his jaw tightening. He took a deep breath and closed his hand around them.

"You girls did the right thing. Now go inside. Stay in the main yard. No wandering. I will handle this."

His tone carried no room for argument.

Emma nodded, but her mind raced. Rusty had not ended up in those woods by accident. Someone had led him there. Someone close enough to keep dropping pieces of equipment along the way. Someone bold enough to return.

As Emma leaned against Rusty's stall later, watching him drift to sleep, she felt the weight of the day settle heavily in her chest.

Rusty was safe now.

But whoever had abandoned him was not finished.

And they were closer than she had imagined.

Chapter Six

Evening settled over Saddle Creek in a slow, deliberate way, as if the sun itself hesitated to leave the ranch behind. Gold seeped across the sky in wide streaks that deepened into rose and violet, and the horses in the paddocks grazed lazily in the warm light. Emma helped Mia stack the last of the brushes in the tack room before heading toward Rusty's stall. The barn felt calmer than it had in days, as if the world had given the three girls a short breath before something else could unfold.

Rusty lay curled on the thick straw with his legs tucked beneath him. His small chest rose and fell in steady rhythm, the peaceful sound making Emma smile. She leaned against the stall rail, her body relaxing after a long, tense day. She felt the air cooling around her as the sun dipped lower, and the rustle of hay in Willow's stall filled the quiet.

Riley approached from the back aisle, her boots scuffing softly along the wooden floor. She stopped a few feet away, glancing briefly at Emma before looking toward Rusty. "He looks better this evening," she said.

Emma nodded. "He ate more today. And he has not wobbled as much."

Riley leaned forward and rested her arms on the stall door, watching the foal with softened eyes. "He trusts you," she said quietly. "He follows you around like you were his mother."

Emma felt warmth bloom in her chest. She rubbed Willow's neck through the bars of the neighboring stall. "I just want him to feel safe."

Riley's eyes flicked to her, thoughtful and unreadable. "I know you do."

They stood in comfortable silence for a moment, listening to the horses settling in for the night. The barn's soft sounds were familiar, steady, grounding. Emma breathed deeply, trying to center herself again after the adrenaline of the fence line discovery.

But peace at Saddle Creek never lasted long.

When Dale shut down the main barn lights, leaving only the soft golden lamps on the outside corners and a warm glow from the feed room, Emma knew it was time to head home. Aunt Sarah would be cooking supper, and Uncle James had planned to show her how to fix a loose hinge on the porch door. But Emma did not feel ready to leave. Something tugged at her, a whisper at the edge of her thoughts that said the night would not pass quietly.

She brushed one more piece of hay off Rusty's ear. "I will see you in the morning," she said softly.

Rusty twitched his tail, kicked lightly, then rested his head again.

Riley walked beside Emma as they headed toward the front gate. The sky had grown darker, streaked with small bands of purple clouds. Fireflies began blinking along the sides of the gravel path, tiny sparks that danced in the rising dusk.

"I hate leaving when the woods feel like this," Riley said suddenly.

Emma nodded, swallowing. "Me too."

Riley glanced at her. "If anything happens, we will figure it out. We always do."

Emma wanted to believe that. She wanted to believe that whatever had brought Rusty into the clearing would not return. But she could not shake the memory of that snap in the woods, the sound of something heavy moving, something that was not an animal.

"It will be okay," Riley said, her voice softer. "You are not alone."

Emma smiled weakly. "Neither are you."

They parted just outside the barn yard. Riley lived only a few minutes away, and Mia had left earlier with her older brother. Emma walked slowly toward her aunt and uncle's house, clutching the strap of her backpack. Gravel crunched beneath her boots. The porch light glowed warmly at the end of the drive, a familiar beacon. But halfway there, she paused.

A shape stood near the fence line. A shadow beside the darkened paddock boundary. Not moving. Tall. Still.

Emma stopped breathing.

She blinked hard. The shape vanished among the trees.

Her heart pounded in her chest, loud and steady. She hurried inside the farmhouse, telling herself it was only her imagination, shadows playing tricks in the fading light.

But the feeling followed her into sleep.

Hours later, something woke her.

A sound.

A sharp one.

A metallic clang, as if a bucket had been struck or a gate had swung too hard. Emma sat upright in bed, heart pounding. The moonlight through her window cast pale blue stripes across the floor. She listened, breath held tight, waiting.

Another sound. Softer. Hooves. Horses moving quickly.

Emma threw off the covers and rushed to the window. The paddocks were dim in the faint moonlight, but she could see silhouettes shifting. Willow was pacing near her fence line, her head raised, ears pricked sharply toward the woods. Storm whinnied from the next paddock, tense and agitated.

Emma felt cold fear crawl up her spine.

Something was wrong.

She grabbed her boots without bothering with socks, slipped her sweater over her pajamas, and hurried downstairs. The old farmhouse creaked under her feet. She did not want to wake her aunt and uncle, and she knew what they would say—stay inside, let Dale handle it in the morning. But Emma could not ignore the horses when they were this distressed. She stepped onto the porch and closed the door quietly behind her.

Night held the ranch in a heavy stillness. The air felt colder now, and a thin layer of mist clung to the ground. Emma could hear the horses clearly. Rustling. Snorting. Hooves shifting restlessly. She ran down the porch steps, her breath visible in the chill night air.

When she reached the paddock fence, Willow bolted toward her, pacing, circling, eyes wide and glimmering in the moonlight. Emma reached through the rails and stroked Willow's neck.

"It is okay," she whispered. "I am here."

But Willow did not calm. She tossed her head, snorted harshly, then stared again toward the line of trees beyond the barn.

Emma's stomach twisted.

A shadow moved between the trunks.

She froze. The movement was too tall, too deliberate. Not a deer. Not a fox. Not anything that belonged there.

Then she heard Rusty.

A terrified, high-pitched cry from inside the barn.

Emma sprinted toward the barn doors. The gravel slid under her boots, and she nearly fell as she stumbled across the threshold. Inside, the barn was dim, lit only by the small night bulb in the feed room. Rusty was on his feet, trembling hard, ears pinned flat against his head. His cry echoed through the rafters, sharp and panicked.

"Rusty," Emma said, rushing into his stall. She wrapped her arms around him, pressing her cheek against his neck. "It is all right. I have you."

But Rusty's trembling did not stop. It grew worse.

A sudden thud outside made Emma jump violently.

Something heavy shifting near the back of the barn.

Another thud. Closer.

Emma looked over her shoulder toward the back doors. They were closed, but a faint shape moved just beyond them, casting a long shadow across the wooden slats.

"Who is there?" Emma whispered, her voice barely audible.

Rusty whimpered.

Then she heard footsteps.

Slow. Deliberate. Moving along the barn wall toward the paddocks.

Emma's breath hitched. She grabbed the stall latch and shut it behind her, hoping the sound would not carry. She stroked Rusty gently, trying to quiet his shivering.

The footsteps paused.

For a moment, complete silence.

Then the barn door latch rattled.

Emma's heart slammed into her ribs.

Someone was trying to open the door.

She clamped a hand over her mouth to stifle a gasp. Rusty pressed into her leg, shaking so hard she worried he would fall over. The latch rattled again, harder this time.

"Emma."

The whisper came from behind her.

She nearly screamed before she recognized the voice.

Riley.

Emma exhaled shakily. Riley stepped out of the shadows near the tack room, eyes wide with fear.

"I saw your light come on," Riley whispered. "Storm woke me up. He was going wild. I thought something happened, so I came back."

Emma swallowed hard. "Someone is outside."

Riley nodded, pale. "I saw something moving along the back paddock."

Another thud sounded outside. Willow screamed, a harsh sound that tore through the night.

Riley's voice trembled. "We have to get out of here."

Emma looked at Rusty. "I am not leaving him."

Riley grabbed her arm. "Emma. We cannot stay."

But something slammed against the back barn doors. Hard. The wood shuddered. Dust fell from the rafters.

Emma stared at the doors, her blood turning cold.

Someone was trying to break in.

Rusty's cries grew desperate. Willow screamed again.

Riley pulled Emma toward the side exit with frantic urgency. Emma resisted. "We cannot leave Rusty."

Riley's voice cracked. "Emma, please."

Another hit against the door. A splinter broke loose.

Emma realized they had seconds, not minutes.

She looked at Riley. Riley's eyes were wide with fear, but also with something else—loyalty. Trust. The kind that said she would not leave without Emma.

Emma gripped Rusty's mane gently. "I am coming back for you," she whispered. "I promise."

Rusty whimpered and pressed his head against her.

Emma forced herself to step away and follow Riley to the side exit. They slipped out the door just as a heavy crash echoed behind them. Riley grabbed Emma's hand and pulled her toward the paddock fence, ducking behind the water trough.

Emma huddled beside her, breath sharp and uneven.

The barn door creaked open.

Someone stepped inside.

The silhouette of a tall figure appeared in the gap. The moonlight behind them cast their shape clearly enough that Emma saw the outline of a coat, broad shoulders, and something glinting in their hand.

Riley's grip on Emma's hand tightened painfully.

The figure paused, scanning the barn interior.

Emma held her breath until her lungs burned.

Then, slowly, the figure turned and walked deeper into the barn.

They were searching.

For Rusty.

Emma's pulse thundered in her ears. She wanted to run to Rusty, to protect him, to scream. But Riley held her down with both hands.

"Do not move," Riley whispered.

Emma nodded, tears burning in her eyes.

The figure moved deeper into the barn. They checked stalls. They walked toward Rusty's stall. Their shadow flickered against the far wall.

Emma's heart broke as she heard Rusty cry again, a terrified sound that echoed through the rafters.

Riley bowed her head, shaking. "We have to get Dale."

Emma nodded weakly. "We cannot leave Rusty alone."

"I know," Riley whispered. "But we cannot fight whoever that is."

Emma forced herself to breathe, each breath jagged, forced.

The figure's footsteps stopped.

Then came a frustrated grunt.

The latch on Rusty's stall rattled.

Emma felt something inside her snap.

She stood.

Riley pulled her back down. "Emma, no."

"He will take Rusty," Emma whispered. "I cannot let him."

Another rattle. A harsh curse from the intruder.

Emma pulled free of Riley's grip and sprinted toward the front of the barn.

"Emma," Riley hissed, scrambling after her.

Emma ignored the terror clawing at her chest. She burst into the open yard, running as fast as she could toward Dale's house. The porch light was off, but she flicked the outside switch desperately, flashing it on and off in frantic signals.

A back door at the farmhand bunkhouse opened. Lights flared. Voices shouted.

Riley reached her seconds later, breath uneven.

Dale came running from behind the equipment shed, coat half buttoned, boots unlaced. "What happened?"

Emma pointed toward the barn, tears streaking her cheeks. "Someone is inside."

Dale's face hardened instantly. He shouted for the ranch hands. Two men grabbed flashlights. Another ran to call the sheriff.

"Stay here," Dale ordered the girls, then sprinted toward the barn.

Emma did not stay.

She ran to the paddock fence instead. Riley caught up and grabbed her sleeve.

Emma's voice shook. "I need to see Rusty."

Riley looked toward the barn. "We will go together."

They approached carefully, staying low behind the trough again. Dale and the ranch hands burst into the barn with flashlights sweeping in large arcs.

"Sheriff is on the way," someone yelled.

Emma's heart raced.

She looked toward the open back doors.

The figure was gone.

Rusty cried again, this time a soft whimper.

Emma ran to the stall. Riley followed. Rusty was pressed against the far wall, trembling, his eyes wide with terror. But he was unharmed.

Emma collapsed to her knees beside him, wrapping her arms around his neck. "It is okay. You are safe. I am here."

Riley's shoulders sagged with relief. "He is all right."

Dale approached them slowly, chest heaving, flashlight in hand. "Whoever it was got away. But they left something."

He held up a glove.

Dark. Heavy. Torn along the palm.

Emma stared at it, her blood cold.

Someone had been inside Rusty's stall.

Someone who knew exactly where to find him.

Dale's voice was grave. "This was not random. Someone came for that foal."

Emma held Rusty tighter.

And for the first time, the danger felt close enough to touch.

Chapter Seven

Emma did not remember falling asleep. One moment she was curled on top of her blanket, boots still on, staring at the faint lines of moonlight across her bedroom ceiling. The next, she was blinking awake to a pale grey light and the quiet ticking of the clock on her nightstand. For a few seconds, she lay still, unsure whether the night before had been real or one of those vivid dreams that stayed with you long after waking.

Then she felt it: the tightness in her chest, the faint ache in her legs from running, the echo of Rusty's terrified cries in her memory.

It had been real.

Emma sat up slowly. Her boots had left faint dust streaks on the quilt, and her sweater was twisted around one shoulder. She had not even bothered to change. Everything from the night came rushing back. Willow's screams from the paddock. The rattling barn door. The tall shadow entering the aisle. Rusty's stall latch shuddering as someone tried it. Dale's flashlight beams cutting through the dark. The sight of that torn glove.

Someone had come for Rusty.

Her hands started to shake. She curled them into fists and took a slow, careful breath. Rusty was safe. That was the first thing she made herself remember. When they had finally gone back into his stall, he had been frightened but unharmed. The intruder had not reached him in time.

She clung to that fact like a small, solid stone in a rushing river.

Footsteps sounded in the hallway outside her room. Her aunt's quiet knock followed a second later.

"Emma? You awake, honey?" Aunt Sarah's voice slid through the door, gentle and concerned.

"Yeah," Emma called back, her voice scratchy. "I am up."

The door opened, and Aunt Sarah stepped inside holding a steaming mug. Her blonde hair was pulled into a messy bun, and there were faint shadows under her eyes, but her expression was soft.

"I figured you might want something warm," she said, handing Emma the mug.

Emma wrapped her hands around it gratefully. The smell of hot chocolate floated up, sweet and familiar. "Thank you."

Her aunt sat on the edge of the bed. "Dale called late last night after you came back in. He told us what happened. You scared us, you know."

"I am sorry," Emma said in a rush. "I know I should have stayed in the house, but the horses were freaking out, and Rusty was screaming, and then someone was inside the barn and I did not know what to do."

"I know," Aunt Sarah said. "And I am not angry. Just worried. That was dangerous."

Emma nodded, her throat thick. "Is the sheriff going to find him?"

"The sheriff will do everything he can," her aunt replied. "He came out after you went back to bed. He and Dale walked the property, checked the fences, looked at the glove. They will check with the nearby ranches. It might take time, but this person is not just going to walk around unnoticed forever."

Emma took a careful sip from the mug. The hot chocolate slid down her throat, warm and steadying. "What about Rusty?"

"He is okay," Aunt Sarah said. "Dale checked on him again just before sunrise. Nervous, but not injured. He said you can come early if you want, once you eat something."

Emma managed a small smile. "I want to go now."

"I figured," her aunt said with a soft laugh. She reached out and brushed a strand of hair away from Emma's face. "Eat a real breakfast first. You will not be any use to Rusty if you pass out in his stall."

Emma nodded, even though part of her wanted to run straight outside. She forced herself to change quickly into clean jeans and a fresh hoodie, washed her face, and went to the kitchen. Uncle James was at the table with a mug of coffee, reading the same article about Pine Hollow that Mia had brought to the barn days ago. He looked up as she entered.

"You heading over to see your colt?" he asked.

"He is not mine," Emma said automatically, though her heart protested the words, "but yes."

Uncle James smiled. "He seems to think you are his."

Her cheeks warmed. "He was really scared last night."

"So were you, I bet," he said.

Emma hesitated, then nodded. "A little."

Her uncle folded the paper and set it aside. "Being scared is not a bad thing. It means you understand something is serious. What matters is what you do while you are scared."

Emma thought about running to flip the porch light on and off, about sprinting for Dale, about going straight to Rusty when she could. "I did not freeze," she said quietly.

"No," Uncle James replied. "You did not."

He pushed a plate toward her. Scrambled eggs, toast, and half a sliced apple. Emma ate quickly, not because she wanted to rush, but because her body suddenly realized how hungry it was. The food settled her, putting a small weight in her stomach that helped anchor her buzzing nerves.

When she finally stepped outside, morning had fully arrived. The sky was bright and clear with soft tufts of cloud drifting lazily overhead. From a distance, Saddle Creek looked peaceful. Birds perched on the fence posts, tails flicking. The paddocks were dotted with grazing horses, their coats glinting in the sunlight. If she had not known about the intruder, she might have believed the ranch was just as safe as it had ever been.

But she knew better now.

She walked quickly down the path. Her boots crunched on the gravel in a steady rhythm that almost matched the pounding of her heart. Every sound made her glance toward the woods. A squirrel launching from one branch to another, a crow lifting off from a fence post, the distant rumble of a truck on the road beyond the ridge. All of it felt sharper, more important, like pieces of a puzzle she did not yet understand.

As she reached the barn, she saw Riley sitting on an overturned bucket just outside the doors. Her elbows were on her knees and her chin rested in her hands. Storm grazed in the nearby paddock, but even from a distance Emma could tell that Riley's eyes were fixed on the barn interior.

She looked tired.

"Hey," Emma said softly as she approached.

Riley looked up. The usual spark of mischief that danced in her eyes when she saw Emma was replaced by something gentler. "You are here," she said. "I was going to come get you if you did not show up soon."

"Is Rusty okay?" Emma asked quickly.

Riley stood. "Come see."

They walked into the barn together. Emma's steps slowed when she saw the back doors. During the night, one of the planks had cracked along the frame. New reinforcement boards were propped beside it, waiting to be installed. The sheriff had dusted the latch with powder, leaving faint white traces along the wood.

Dale had done his best to make everything feel normal again, but the marks were still there. A reminder.

Rusty's stall, however, looked different. Someone had added a second latch higher on the door, and a small chain was looped through both latches for extra security. A fleece blanket had been draped over the back half of the stall rail, creating a cosier corner. Rusty stood beneath it, his head peeking out, ears pricked when he saw Emma.

He whickered softly.

Emma's chest eased. She stepped inside the stall and reached for him. He pressed his nose into her shoulder and leaned against her so hard she nearly lost her balance. His body vibrated with a fine tremor. He lifted one hoof and set it down again, restless and anxious.

"I know," Emma whispered. "Last night was scary. I was scared too."

Riley leaned on the stall door. "He did not sleep much. He kept waking up every time a board creaked."

Emma looked over her shoulder at her. "Did you stay with him?"

Riley shrugged, trying to look casual. "For a while."

"How long is a while?" Emma asked.

Riley shifted her weight. "Until about three. Maybe four."

Emma stared. "Riley."

"What?" Riley demanded, her cheeks coloring. "I could not sleep either. Storm was pacing and snorting. I figured someone should be here in case that creep came back. Dale was out with the sheriff for part of the night. It would have been stupid to leave him alone."

Emma felt warmth spread through her chest. "You are not stupid."

"Good," Riley said, though her mouth twitched like she was fighting a smile, "because I am really tired."

Emma laughed softly. Rusty nuzzled her neck and then Riley's hand where it rested on the stall door, as if agreeing.

"You did not have to stay," Emma said.

"I know," Riley replied. This time she did not try to hide her small smile. "But I wanted to."

They fell into a quiet rhythm, tending to Rusty together. Emma mixed his morning mash with careful portions while Riley checked his legs for any signs of strain from the previous night's panic. Mia arrived shortly after, carrying a bundle of fresh straw and looking rumpled, her braid slightly crooked.

"You guys look like you have been awake for hours," she said, dropping the straw by the stall.

"We kind of have," Riley said.

Mia frowned at Rusty's wide eyes. "Poor baby. Did the sheriff say anything?"

"Not much yet," Riley answered. "They are going to check nearby properties today. Dale said they think the intruder took off toward the old service road."

"Whoever it was knew where Rusty is," Emma added. "They went straight to the back of the barn."

Mia shivered. "That is creepy."

"It means we are doing the right thing by keeping him here," Riley said. "At least we know he is protected."

Protected. The word felt fragile in Emma's mind. But as she watched Rusty begin to nibble at his mash, as she felt the warmth of his breath on her hand, she decided to cling to it anyway.

Dr. Huxley arrived midmorning. His truck pulled into the driveway with a familiar rumble. He walked in with his leather bag, his expression serious but not alarmed. Dale joined them by Rusty's stall as the vet stepped inside to examine the colt.

"Well," Dr. Huxley said, running a practiced hand along Rusty's neck, "someone had quite an adventure last night."

Rusty tensed at the unknown touch, but Emma's hand on his shoulder calmed him. The colt glanced back at her, and she nodded reassuringly. He stood still, though one ear remained turned uncertainly toward the vet.

"His heart rate is a bit elevated," Dr. Huxley noted, listening with his stethoscope. "But nothing dangerous. It is to be expected after what happened."

"Can fear hurt him long term?" Emma asked quietly.

"Not if it is followed by safety," the vet replied. He gave her a kind look. "Animals are like people, Emma. The bad memories stay, but they can be covered by enough good ones that they stop hurting so much."

Riley shifted closer to the stall door. "Can you tell anything more about where he came from?"

Dr. Huxley hesitated, then ran his hand along Rusty's neck again, lifting the mane to inspect the coat beneath. He traced his fingers gently over the small white star on Rusty's forehead and down along the crooked line of the colt's jaw.

"I made some calls," he said. "I spoke with an inspector who visited Pine Hollow last month, and with another vet who has treated horses from that property and a few neighboring ones. There is a pattern."

"What kind of pattern?" Dale asked.

"The foals from one particular outfit tend to share a certain look," Dr. Huxley answered. "They breed for a specific ring style. Clean legs, refined heads, a particular shoulder shape. Rusty's conformation is very similar. Also, one of the barns in question has a habit of moving foals with minor imperfections quietly. They sometimes sell them through small sale barns without much paperwork."

Riley frowned. "Like the crooked jaw."

"Yes," Dr. Huxley said. "A foal like Rusty would not match their sale brochure photos. He would not bring in the highest price. To the wrong person, that makes him disposable."

Emma's hand tightened on Rusty's shoulder. "That is awful."

"It is," Dr. Huxley agreed. "But this tells us something important. Whoever abandoned him likely did not see him as a pet or a companion. They saw him as a problem. And when someone sees an animal as a problem, they often come back if they think that problem might expose them."

"Like last night," Riley said quietly.

Dr. Huxley nodded. "Exactly. The sheriff asked me to pass along anything I learned that might help. He is going to pay a visit to that outfit later this week."

Emma looked at Rusty, who had finished his mash and now leaned more heavily into her side, his eyes half closed. "What happens to him?" she asked. "If they find out where he came from. Will they make him go back?"

Dale rested a hand on her shoulder. "No one is sending him anywhere he is not safe. Not if I have anything to say about it."

"Or me," Riley added.

"Or me," Mia said quickly.

Dr. Huxley smiled. "The sheriff will do everything by the book, but the law does not always favor people who abandon vulnerable animals. Especially not when there is evidence they tried to break into a barn at night."

Emma took a breath of relief she did not realize she had been holding. Rusty nuzzled her arm, then took a small, hesitant step away from her. His ears flicked forward, and he lifted his head as if suddenly curious about the rest of the stall.

"Look at that," the vet said. "Energy is coming back. That is good."

"He is still scared of sudden noises," Emma said. "But he is braver than he was."

"Then help him be braver," Dr. Huxley replied. "Routine. Gentle challenges. Let him move a little more today. Not too much, but enough that he remembers his legs can carry him."

Dale nodded. "We can set up a small pen in the indoor arena after lessons. Give him space to explore without risk."

Emma's pulse quickened. "Can I help?"

"I was hoping you would," Dale said.

Riley leaned against the stall rail, her expression brightening. "Me too."

Mia grinned. "Obviously I am not missing that."

The plan settled around them like a promise.

For the rest of the morning, the ranch hummed with normal activity. Students arrived for riding lessons, parents chatted near the viewing arena, and horses flicked their tails at flies. The sheriff stopped by briefly to talk to Dale and take the glove back to the station, along with photographs of the broken door and the hoofprints near the woods. Emma watched from a distance, trying not to stare but unable to look away completely. The sight of the patrol car parked in the gravel lane made the whole thing feel more real somehow, like something out of a show she might have watched, except this was her barn, her horses, her foal.

By late afternoon, the lesson horses had been cooled out and returned to their stalls. The indoor arena was quiet and empty, its sandy floor freshly dragged into smooth, even lines. Sunlight filtered through the high windows, casting soft rectangles of light on the dirt.

Dale helped set up a temporary pen using lightweight panels at one end of the arena. It formed a square enclosure large enough for Rusty to walk, turn, and maybe even trot a few steps if he felt bold, but small enough that he would not become overwhelmed.

Emma led Rusty from the barn toward the arena with a short lead clipped to his halter. He walked beside her more confidently now, ears flicking back and forth as he took in the new sights and smells. Riley walked on Rusty's other side, ready to steady him if he spooked. Mia carried a small bucket of grain and a few carrot pieces as rewards.

Rusty hesitated at the arena entrance, sniffing the edge of the doorway. His hooves made a different sound on the packed earth just inside, and he lifted his head uncertainly.

"It is okay," Emma said in a calm, low voice. "This is a good place. Horses work here. You will like it."

Riley kept her tone light. "Promise there are no creepy strangers in here. Just us."

Rusty flicked an ear toward her, then took another small step forward. As they led him into the pen, his muscles tensed for a moment, but he did not pull away. The high ceiling and open space echoed the sound of his hooves and the soft scuff of their boots, but otherwise the arena felt quiet.

Emma unlatched the lead rope and held it loosely in her hand, giving Rusty the freedom to move while remaining close enough to catch him if he panicked. For a long moment, he stayed at her side, pressed against her hip, eyes wide. Then curiosity finally nudged aside some of his fear.

He took one step forward on his own.

Then another.

Emma watched him with a mixture of awe and fear. He walked to the far end of the pen and sniffed the panel, then looked back over his shoulder as if checking to make sure she was still there.

"I am here," Emma said. "Go on. Explore."

Rusty lowered his head, sniffed the dirt, and pawed once, sending up a small puff of dust. He sneezed at it, which made Mia giggle, and the sound echoed faintly in the high rafters.

"That was kind of cute," Mia whispered.

"It was," Riley agreed, a smile tugging at her mouth.

Rusty moved around the pen slowly, stopping every few steps to look back at Emma. Each time she met his gaze and nodded encouragingly. He completed one small circle, then another, his steps gradually becoming smoother, more confident.

"He is doing so well," Emma murmured.

"Let us see if he will follow your cue now," Dale said from the rail. He had been watching quietly, arms folded, his expression thoughtful and proud. "Walk a few steps away. See if he goes with you without the rope."

Emma swallowed and stepped toward the center of the pen. Rusty paused, ears flicking. She clicked her tongue softly and patted her thigh.

"Come on, Rusty," she said. "You can do it."

For a heartbeat, he did not move. Then he stepped toward her. Slowly, carefully, but without hesitation in his eyes. When he reached her, he bumped his nose gently against her hand, as if asking if this had been the right choice.

Emma's heart swelled. She rubbed his forehead. "That is my brave boy."

"Try walking in a circle," Dale suggested.

Emma took a few steps to her right. Rusty followed, staying just behind her shoulder, the way a well trained horse would follow a lead in the ring. His hooves made soft prints in the sand beside her footprints. They traced a careful arc across the pen. On the second circle, Rusty's head dropped a little lower, his ears relaxed, and his stride lengthened. Emma felt his tension easing through the lead rope, which now hung almost slack between them.

Riley leaned on the rail, her eyes shining. "Look at them. He is really doing it."

Mia rested her chin on her arms. "He trusts her completely."

"Try a change of direction," Dale said. "Gently."

Emma stopped and turned toward Rusty. She stepped backward, guiding him with a slight motion of her hand. Rusty hesitated only a heartbeat before turning with her, his body curving as he changed direction. They traced another circle, this time moving the opposite way. The movement was not perfect, not as polished as an older, trained horse, but it was clear and deliberate. Rusty was not stumbling anymore. He was choosing to move, to listen, to stay with her.

Emma felt a prickling behind her eyes. She blinked it away, focusing on the pattern of their steps.

Around and around.

Slow and steady.

Together.

After a while, she stopped and patted Rusty's neck. "You are amazing," she whispered. "So brave."

Rusty blew out a long breath, a soft, contented sound that made Emma's chest ache in the best way.

Mia passed a carrot piece through the rail. "Reward time."

Emma offered it to Rusty. He snuffed it for a moment, then took it carefully from her hand and chewed with obvious pleasure.

"You just made a big step today," Emma said softly. "You remembered that you do not always have to be afraid."

Riley hopped down from the rail and joined them in the pen. "Can I try something?" she asked.

Emma nodded and stepped back. Riley approached Rusty slowly, hand outstretched, palm up. Rusty sniffed it, then bumped her fingers as if asking whether she had another carrot.

"Sorry, buddy, Mia has the snacks," Riley said. She ran her hand along his neck, then moved quietly to his side. "Let us see if you will follow both of us."

She and Emma stood a few feet apart, forming a small angle. One at Rusty's head, one by his shoulder. Together they walked forward in a gentle curve. Rusty followed, walking between them. When he faltered, Emma spoke to him. When he flinched at a small creak from the rafters, Riley murmured something soothing.

They moved as a trio, their steps gradually falling into a shared rhythm.

"You two look like you have been practicing," Mia teased from the rail.

Emma smiled, feeling something loosen that had been tight since the night he appeared in the woods. This was what she loved about Saddle Creek. The way one frightened horse could become part of something bigger. The way people and animals learned to move together.

This was why she could not bear the thought of anyone taking Rusty away.

After another few minutes, Dale signaled for them to stop. "That is enough for today. End on a good note. We do not want to tire him out."

Emma nodded and led Rusty back to the center of the pen. She rubbed his forehead again and leaned her cheek briefly against his neck. He smelled like clean dust, warm coat, and a faint trace of hay. His heartbeat under her ear was steady.

"You did great," she whispered. "We will do more tomorrow."

As they led Rusty back to the barn, Willow called softly from her stall, her ears pricking with interest. Emma glanced at her and saw the mare's eyes focused on Rusty with surprising gentleness. When they reached her stall, Rusty paused, looking up at her as if drawn by some quiet thread.

Willow lowered her head and snuffed at him through the bars, making a low, rumbling sound deep in her chest. It was not a warning. It was comforting. Rusty stood still, eyes half closed, leaning slightly into the contact. For a moment, the world outside the barn seemed to disappear. No intruders. No broken doors. No hoofprints in the woods.

Just the soft sound of a mare soothing a foal who had seen too much.

Riley watched with an oddly tender expression. "Maybe he picked the right herd," she said.

Emma smiled. "I think so."

Later, after Rusty had been settled back into his stall with fresh water and a soft bed of straw, Emma and Riley sat together on the rail of the empty arena, legs swinging lazily over the sand.

"You were really brave last night," Riley said suddenly, staring out at the quiet space.

Emma blinked. "I was terrified."

"Me too," Riley admitted. "But you still ran for help. You still came back for Rusty as soon as it was safe. I almost could not move when I saw that guy's shadow in the barn."

"You held me back when I wanted to run straight toward him," Emma said. "That was brave too."

Riley gave a small huff of laughter. "I do not know if that was bravery or self preservation."

"Both," Emma said. "You always say we are a team. That is what we were."

Riley's shoulders softened. "Yeah. I guess we were."

A comfortable silence settled between them. Sunshine filtered through the high arena windows, striping the sand with light. Dust motes floated lazily in the air.

"Do you think things will go back to normal?" Emma asked quietly.

Riley sat with the question for a moment before answering. "I do not think they will go back to the way they were before we found Rusty. But maybe they will make a new kind of normal. One where he is safe here, no matter who tries to take him."

Emma let those words wrap around her like a warm blanket.

A new normal.

One where she was not the new girl anymore, but part of something that had roots.

One where a frightened foal who had been thrown away by someone else could learn that he mattered at Saddle Creek.

One where shadows in the woods did not get to decide the story.

"Whatever happens," Emma said, "we will protect him."

Riley nodded, her mouth set in a determined line. "Together."

The word settled deep inside Emma's chest, steady and sure.

She looked toward the barn where Rusty dozed in his stall, Willow standing quietly nearby, ears tilted in his direction. The ranch was not entirely safe, not with someone still out there who wanted to erase a mistake by taking him back or making him disappear. But for the first time since the intruder crept into the barn, Emma felt something stronger than fear take hold.

Hope.

Rusty had taken his first brave steps that day.

So had they.

The danger was not gone.

But now, they were moving toward it with their eyes open, hearts steady, and a little foal who had finally remembered how to walk forward.

And somewhere in the distant woods, out of sight and just beyond hearing, unseen eyes might still be watching the ranch.

Yet inside the barn, surrounded by friends and horses, Emma knew one thing for certain.

Whoever that person was, whatever their plans had been, they had not counted on Rusty finding a girl who would not give up, a prickly friend who stood her ground, and a ranch that protected its own.

That, she thought as she hopped off the rail and headed back toward the barn, was their greatest advantage of all.

Chapter Eight

Morning came with a soft grey haze that clung low over the fields like a blanket not yet ready to be pulled away. Emma walked down the gravel path toward the barn with her hands shoved deep into her hoodie pockets. She tried to breathe steadily, but her chest felt tight. Even the familiar smell of hay and cedar could not fully chase away the uneasiness that lingered after the night of the intruder.

Her dreams had been restless. In one, she had reached Rusty only to find his stall empty. In another, Willow had bolted into the woods while shadows chased them both. She knew dreams did not always mean anything, but they had left her with a weight she could not shake.

The barn door creaked open as she stepped inside. The light was warm and golden, pooling along the floorboards. Rusty stood with his head over the stall rail, ears pricked forward. He let out a soft nicker when he saw her.

Emma's heart lifted a little. She hurried forward and rubbed his soft forehead. "Good morning, brave boy."

Rusty pressed his nose so hard into her chest it nearly knocked her backwards. She laughed quietly. "You slept better, didn't you?"

"Only because someone checked on him twice in the night," Riley said from behind her.

Emma turned. Riley stood leaning against Storm's stall door, sipping from a travel mug. Her braid was neat today, which usually meant she was trying to act like she had everything under control. But Emma noticed the faint tiredness in her eyes.

"You checked on him again?" Emma asked.

Riley shrugged. "Could not sleep. Storm was grumpy and kept stomping. I figured I might as well make sure the doors had not walked away in the night."

Emma smiled. "Thank you."

Riley waved a hand. "Do not make a big deal."

But Emma knew it was a big deal. Riley guarded her feelings like a dragon guarding treasure. For her to spend the night checking on Rusty meant she cared more than she wanted to admit.

Mia entered the barn with a bag of fresh carrots. "Breakfast delivery," she announced. She held up a carrot stick toward Rusty, who stretched eagerly toward it.

Emma laughed. "He likes you too much."

"He likes food," Mia replied. "I just happen to bring it."

They fed Rusty, cleaned his stall, and spent a few minutes brushing him. Everything looked normal. Peaceful, even. For a moment, Emma let herself relax.

Then Willow slammed her hoof against her stall wall.

Emma jumped.

Willow tossed her head, snorting sharply. Her tail swished in agitation, and she paced in a tight circle.

"Something is bothering her," Emma said.

Riley frowned. "That is not normal morning Willow."

Emma walked toward Willow slowly. "Hey girl, what is wrong?"

Willow pinned her ears for half a second, then flicked them

forward again. She stretched her neck and stared toward the back of the barn.

Emma followed her gaze.

The back doors had been repaired, freshly hammered boards reinforcing the broken frame. Everything looked orderly and secure. No shadows moved there. No one lurked nearby.

But Willow did not stop staring.

Emma felt the uneasiness creep back under her skin.

"Maybe she remembers last night," Mia suggested.

"Maybe," Emma replied softly. But something about Willow's posture made her think there was more. As if the mare sensed something the humans could not see.

Riley rubbed Storm's neck. "Let us get through the morning chores. Dale wants us to help set up the outdoor arena after lunch."

Emma nodded. She forced herself to focus. They fed the horses, cleaned buckets, swept aisles, and organized tack for the afternoon lesson riders. The routine helped settle Emma's nerves. Routine always did.

But the quiet did not last.

After chores, Dale pulled the three girls aside. His brow was furrowed more deeply than usual.

"The sheriff called with an update," he said.

Emma felt her stomach clench.

Riley crossed her arms. "What did he say?"

"They visited the place Dr. Huxley mentioned," Dale replied. "The owner denied everything, said they have never lost a foal and have perfect records."

Mia made a face. "Do they expect us to believe that?"

Dale sighed. "People lie when they think they can get away with it. The sheriff is not convinced either. He is waiting for a warrant to check the property more thoroughly."

"Did they ask about the intruder?" Emma asked.

"They did," Dale said. "The owner claims he has no idea who would do such a thing. Which does not mean much. But the sheriff thinks whoever came here last night is someone who knows their way around horses. Someone strong enough to break that door and quick enough to get away."

Emma swallowed. The image of the tall shadow flooded her mind again.

Riley's jaw tightened. "Well, they are not getting Rusty."

"No," Dale said. "They are not. But we are not letting our guard down. I want the three of you to stick together today. Do not wander off alone. Understood?"

They all nodded.

Emma tried to ignore the cold knot that formed in her stomach.

They headed to the outdoor arena after lunch. Rusty remained in the barn with a new camera Dale had set up watching his stall. The sheriff had loaned them the small motion sensor device.

Emma tried to breathe deeply as she walked Willow out for an easy warm up before lessons started. The mare moved stiffly at first, her muscles tight, her eyes wide. Emma felt her uneasiness spike.

"It is okay," Emma murmured. "We are safe."

But Willow flicked an ear toward the woods, her steps becoming jumpy.

Riley led Storm into the arena behind her. "Willow's acting strange."

"I know," Emma said. "She won't relax."

"Maybe she senses something," Riley replied.

Emma bit her lip. "Like what?"

Riley hesitated. "I do not know."

Mia set up poles along the far end of the arena. "Well, the faster we finish, the faster we can get back to Rusty."

Emma nodded and tried to focus. She mounted Willow and began a slow walk around the arena. Willow's ears flicked constantly, her steps uneven. Emma held the reins lightly, giving her space but keeping her steady.

"Easy girl," she whispered.

But Willow suddenly stiffened.

Emma felt it instantly.

The mare's muscles coiled under her like a loaded spring.

"No, no, no," Emma whispered.

Willow spooked.

She jumped sideways, nearly unseating Emma. Sand kicked up behind them. Emma clung to the reins, heart racing, trying to steady her breath.

"Sit back," Riley called. "Give her support."

Emma tried, but her hands trembled. She felt the fear from the night echo through her body, rising like a wave she could not control.

Willow felt it too.

She scooted forward, head high.

Emma's heart hammered in her chest.

"I cannot," Emma whispered.

Riley jumped into the arena and grabbed Willow's bridle, slowing the mare to a stop. "It is okay. You are okay."

Willow snorted hard, sides heaving.

Emma slid off, her legs shaking.

"Are you all right?" Riley asked.

Emma nodded weakly, though the truth sat heavy on her tongue. "She does not trust me today."

Riley touched her shoulder. "You are shaken. She is just reacting to you."

Emma looked away. "I thought I was getting past it."

"Last night was terrifying," Riley said gently. "It is normal to be nervous."

"But what if I make things worse?" Emma whispered.

"You will not," Riley said.

Emma wanted to believe her.

But Willow still pawed at the ground, unsettled.

And Emma felt the sting of failure crawl under her skin.

. . .

After getting Willow settled, they returned to the barn to check on Rusty. Emma hoped his quiet presence would help steady her again.

But Rusty was not quiet.

He was pacing.

His ears flicked sharply. His eyes were wide. He kept stopping at the back of the stall and staring toward the barn's rear doors.

Emma felt her breath catch. "What is wrong now?"

Mia pointed toward the floor. "Look."

A trail of dirt.

Fresh dirt.

It led from the back door to Rusty's stall.

As if someone had stepped inside the barn again.

Emma's heart slammed into her ribs. "No. We locked those doors."

"We did," Riley said. Her voice shook. "Someone opened them."

Emma followed the trail with her eyes. It ended at the corner post near Rusty's stall. Something small glinted there.

She crouched.

A small metal ring lay in the dirt.

Not a ring for a finger.

A ring used for horse tack.

A lead rope ring.

Rusty whimpered.

Emma's hands trembled as she picked it up. "Someone dropped this. Someone got close."

Dale rushed in from the side aisle. "I just got off the phone with the sheriff. They have a lead."

Emma turned sharply. "What kind of lead?"

Dale hesitated. "Someone matching the intruder's description was spotted near the county road late last night. Walking fast. Holding something."

"What something?" Riley asked.

"A lead rope," Dale answered.

Emma stared at Rusty.

Rusty stared back, trembling.

"He was coming for him," Emma whispered.

"Not happening," Dale said firmly. "Not on my watch."

But the fear was already pooling cold and heavy in Emma's stomach.

The intruder was still close.

Still searching.

Still determined.

The training breakthrough from yesterday felt suddenly fragile, like a glass figurine knocked to the edge of a shelf.

And Emma could not escape the horrible thought rising inside her.

What if it was her fault Rusty was in danger?

What if the intruder came back because Rusty had bonded with her?

Because she had found him first?

The fear grew stronger. Deep. Tangling. Choking.

Rusty nickered softly, pressing his head against her shoulder.

Emma held him tight, but tears stung her eyes.

"I am so sorry," she whispered. "I do not know if I can keep you safe."

Riley stepped beside her quietly.

"You already are," Riley said softly. "You saved him once. And we will save him again."

Emma wiped her eyes with the back of her sleeve. "But everything keeps going wrong."

"That is what happens before things go right," Riley replied, her voice steady. "We do not give up."

Mia nodded, stepping closer. "Emma, he is scared because of what happened. Not because of you."

Emma swallowed. Rusty leaned into her again.

She closed her eyes.

No matter how frightened she was, no matter how many setbacks came, she could not let the fear take over.

Rusty needed her.

And she needed him.

She opened her eyes slowly. "Okay," she whispered. "We keep going."

Riley smiled. "Good. Because I am not letting you run away."

Emma managed a small laugh. "Would not get far anyway."

Dale stepped forward. "We tighten security tonight. No one is going near this barn without me knowing."

Emma nodded. She lifted Rusty's head gently into her arms.

She was still scared.

Still shaken.

But somewhere beneath all the fear and all the doubt was a small spark warming in her ribs.

Determination.

Chapter Seven had brought hope.

Chapter Eight brought a storm.

But now Emma understood something important.

Hope meant nothing unless you kept fighting for it.

And she would.

For Rusty.

For Willow.

For the ranch that had become her home.

And for herself.

Chapter Nine

The next morning arrived with a brilliant sunrise that felt almost dishonest. After everything that had happened, Emma expected the world to reflect the tension she carried inside her. Instead, the sky blazed with streaks of orange and coral, soft clouds drifting slowly across the horizon like nothing bad had ever touched Saddle Creek Ranch.

Emma walked down the gravel path with a knot sitting square in the middle of her stomach. The events of the last two days had woven themselves into her thoughts until she could barely separate fear from determination. She had not slept well. Every small sound outside her window had made her sit upright in bed, expecting to see movement near the fence line or the silhouette of a person in the yard.

Her boots crunched on the gravel, the familiar sound steadying her a little. She rounded the corner and saw Dale already standing beside the barn doors. His arms were crossed over his chest, and he was staring across the pasture toward the woods, the way someone stared at something they could not quite see but definitely felt.

"Morning," Emma said, though her voice came out softer than she intended.

Dale looked over at her and nodded. "Morning. Girls are already inside. Thought you might want to check on Rusty first thing."

Emma nodded and hurried into the barn. Riley and Mia stood near Rusty's stall while Willow pawed anxiously inside hers. The tension in the barn felt sharp, not loud but intense, the kind of unsettled quiet that lived in the air after a storm.

Rusty did not lift his head over the stall rail the way he usually did. Emma stepped closer and found him standing in the far corner. His eyes were wide, and his sides rose and fell too quickly.

"Hey, boy," she said, her voice trembling at the sight of him. "What is wrong?"

Rusty did not move. He looked past her, toward the back of the barn.

Emma's heart tightened. "Did something happen?"

Mia stepped forward. "We found the back doors cracked open again."

Emma turned sharply. "What? I thought Dale locked them."

"He did," Riley said. "He checked them himself last night. But this morning they were open about an inch."

Emma felt a chill slide up her spine. "Did someone come back?"

"We do not know," Riley answered quietly. "Storm was unsettled too. When I came in he would not stop staring toward the woods."

Emma reached into the stall and rubbed Rusty's neck. He leaned into her hand as if clinging to the only safe thing he knew.

"Is the sheriff coming back?" Emma asked.

"Already here," Riley said. "He is outside talking to Dale."

Emma nodded. Her pulse raced.

"Can I go see?" she asked.

Riley hesitated. "Maybe later. Let us stay with Rusty for a minute."

Emma reluctantly agreed. Rusty's breath gradually slowed, though the tension in his body stayed. Willow kept pacing at the stall divider, her hooves clacking softly on the wood.

Emma looked from Willow to Rusty. "They know something," she whispered. "They can feel it."

Mia folded her arms tightly. "I hate this. Why can this person not leave Rusty alone?"

"Because they think he belongs to them," Riley said through clenched teeth. "And they are wrong."

Emma's chest ached. She wanted desperately to believe Rusty was safe now, that Saddle Creek would protect him, that someone like Dale would never let harm come to him. But the fear stuck like a thorn under her skin.

After a few quiet minutes, Dale called them from the barn entrance. "Girls," he said, "come here a moment."

Emma squeezed Rusty once more, then followed Riley and Mia outside. The sheriff stood near the paddock fence, his hands on his hips as he studied the line of trees.

"What is happening?" Emma asked.

The sheriff turned toward her. He had a calm, measured face, the kind that felt reassuring even in tense moments. "We found something this morning," he said. "Something you should know about."

Emma's stomach twisted. "What did you find?"

The sheriff pointed to the ground near the fence. "Someone walked through here last night. Fresh prints. A bootprint. We matched the tread pattern to the one near the barn door from the break-in."

Emma's breath caught. "So it is the same person."

"Yes," the sheriff said. "And there is more." He pointed toward the woods. "We found hoofprints."

Riley stiffened. "Rusty did not leave the barn."

"These are much larger," the sheriff said. "A full-size horse. Someone rode in close, dismounted, and walked toward the barn."

Emma felt her heart pounding. "They came on horseback."

"Yes," he said. "Quietly. Which means they know the property, and they know how to avoid noise."

Emma pressed a hand to her chest. Her breath felt thin. "They tried again."

"We believe so," the sheriff confirmed. "You all need to be extra cautious."

"Did you see where they went?" Riley asked.

"They rode along the old creek trail," he replied. "Toward the far pasture. Then the tracks disappear in the rocky patch."

Emma looked toward the woods. The dark pines loomed silently, their trunks tall and still. She felt something watching. Or maybe she imagined it. She could not tell anymore.

"Girls," Dale said, "I want all three of you helping in pairs today. No one goes anywhere alone."

Even though his voice was firm, Emma could hear worry beneath it.

"We understand," Emma said.

The sheriff nodded and turned back toward the trees. "Let me know if anything else looks strange. Even small things."

Dale walked him toward the farmhouse. Riley let out a shaky breath.

"I do not like this," she said. "I feel like he is watching the ranch."

Emma looked toward the woods again. The branches moved gently in the breeze. But it felt purposeful somehow.

Like the trees were holding secrets.

By midmorning the barn had settled into a tentative routine. Rusty was calmer now, though still alert. They fed him, cleaned his stall again, and set up small enrichment activities for him: a hanging apple, a tiny soft ball, a handful of hay scattered for foraging. He interacted with them all cautiously, but it was a sign that he wanted to move again.

When the riding lesson students began arriving after lunch, Emma volunteered to help Riley set out cones and poles in the lower arena. She wanted to keep busy. Her mind buzzed with fear every time she stood still for too long.

But as they finished placing the last pole, Dale approached with a phone in his hand and a grim expression.

"Emma," he called, "come here, please."

Emma's heart jumped. She jogged toward him. Riley did too.

"What is wrong?" Emma asked.

"I just received a call from Dr. Huxley," Dale said. "He asked if Rusty was with you girls."

Emma blinked. "What? He is in the barn."

Dale shook his head. "No. He is not."

Emma froze.

"What do you mean he is not?" she whispered.

"I checked twenty minutes ago," Dale said. "He was there then. When Dr. Huxley called just now, I told him he was fine, but I sent someone to look, and they could not find him."

Emma's heart slammed into her ribs.

"No," she said, shaking her head. "He cannot be gone. He cannot."

"Let us go," Riley said, grabbing Emma's arm.

They ran.

Emma's legs barely touched the ground as she sprinted toward the barn. Every nightmare, every fear, every image of Rusty alone in the woods rushed into her head. Her breath came sharp and fast. She threw herself inside the barn, nearly colliding with the stall door.

She looked into Rusty's stall.

Empty.

The straw was disturbed. A bucket had tipped onto its side. Emma's entire body went cold. She felt her vision tunnel.

"No," she whispered. "No, no, no."

Riley and Mia ran in behind her.

Mia gasped. "He is gone?"

Emma gripped the stall rail so hard her knuckles turned white. "He cannot be gone."

"Look," Riley said sharply, pointing to the ground. "Here."

A small patch of sand near the stall door was disturbed, marked by what looked like a dragging hoof. Not a large horse. A small one.

Rusty.

Emma rushed to the tack room door. It was slightly ajar.

"He went through here," she said. "He must have been spooked."

Riley moved ahead, scanning the ground. "Look. More tracks."

Small hoofprints led toward the feed room.

Emma followed them, her heart in her throat.

She pushed the feed room door open.

"Rusty?" she called.

Something shifted inside.

Emma rushed forward, nearly tripping over a stack of grain bags.

Then she saw him.

Rusty stood pressed tight against the wall behind a plastic storage bin, trembling but unharmed.

Emma nearly collapsed with relief.

"Oh thank goodness," she whispered. "Rusty."

She approached slowly so she did not frighten him again. Rusty stepped forward and pressed into her chest so suddenly she let out a soft cry.

Emma wrapped her arms around his neck. "You scared me so much," she murmured. "Do not run off like that."

He whimpered softly, burying his nose in her hoodie.

Riley placed a hand on her shoulder. "False alarm, but he was scared."

Mia nodded. "He must have heard something."

Emma froze.

"What did he hear?" she whispered.

The feed room window was cracked open slightly. A faint breeze stirred the plastic curtains. Emma walked to the window and peered out.

There, in the soft dirt just beneath the sill, was a fresh bootprint.

Large.

Deep.

And right under the open window.

Riley sucked in a breath. "Emma..."

Emma's heart fell into her stomach.

"He was here," Emma said. "Whoever it is. He was right outside the barn again."

Rusty whinnied softly, pressing closer against her.

Emma held him tightly. The fear inside her twisted into something else.

Something stronger.

Something fierce.

"No one is taking you," she said quietly to Rusty. "Not ever."

She turned to Riley and Mia.

"We need to find out who this is," she said. "We need the whole truth."

Riley nodded slowly. "We will."

Mia swallowed hard. "What do we do now?"

Emma lifted her chin.

"We look for clues," she said. "We tell Dale and the sheriff. And we stay together."

Her voice did not shake.

She felt the shift inside her clearly.

Fear had ruled her for too long.

Now determination was rising, steady and solid.

Rusty looked up at her with wide, trusting eyes.

Emma stroked his soft forehead. "I am not giving up."

Outside the barn, the trees stood still in the sunlight, tall and quiet.

But somewhere under their shadows, someone had stood that morning. Close enough to see Rusty's stall. Close enough to reach inside the feed room window.

Emma did not know who they were.

But she knew one thing with absolute certainty.

The Lost Foal Mystery (Young adult horse fiction)

They were not done.
And neither was she.

Chapter Ten

The next day felt heavier from the moment Emma opened her eyes. The sky outside her window was a flat pale blue, empty of clouds, but the light seemed thinner somehow, like the sun was having trouble pushing through something invisible. She lay still for a while, staring at the ceiling and letting her thoughts catch up with her.

Rusty in the feed room, shaking behind the bins.

The bootprint under the window.

The open back doors.

The hoofprints by the fence.

All of it pressed inside her chest like stones.

She sat up slowly and swung her feet to the floor. Her boots waited where she had left them, lined up beside one another as if they understood that she would need them again, that the day ahead would demand both courage and steadiness. She pulled on jeans and a clean sweatshirt, tied her hair back, and hurried down the hall.

Her aunt was already in the kitchen, sliding pancakes off a pan onto a plate. The smell of butter and syrup filled the room. It should have been comforting. It almost was.

"Morning, sweetheart," Aunt Sarah said. "You look tired."

"I am okay," Emma answered, though she knew her aunt could hear the strain under the words.

Aunt Sarah nodded toward the table. "Sit. Eat. Dale called early. He asked you to come to the house first, not the barn. The sheriff is stopping by, and they want to talk to you girls together."

Emma's pulse jumped. "Did they find something?"

"I think so," her aunt said. "He did not say everything on the phone, but his voice sounded... different. Focused."

Emma sat and forced herself to eat a few bites of pancake even though her stomach felt too knotted for food. The syrup tasted sweet and familiar, like a piece of her old life before all of this, before intruders and hoofprints and abandoned foals.

"Do you think Rusty will be okay?" she asked quietly.

"I do," Aunt Sarah said. "He has you. And he has an entire ranch full of people who are ready to stand between him and anyone who wants to hurt him."

Emma swallowed the lump in her throat. "Sometimes it still feels like we might lose him."

"Sometimes things feel like that right before they turn around," her aunt said. "Just remember you are not the only one fighting for him."

When she finished breakfast, she walked quickly toward the main ranch house. The air was cool, with a faint breeze that rippled the grass in the paddocks. Birds flitted from fence post to fence post, and she caught sight of Storm tossing his head playfully in his field. Riley stood near the porch steps, hands in her pockets, shoulders hunched against the wind.

"Hey," Emma said as she approached.

Riley lifted her head. "You too, huh?"

"Dale called you?" Emma asked.

"Yeah," Riley replied. "Said the sheriff has news."

Mia arrived a few minutes later, jogging up the path with her braid half coming loose and her cheeks flushed. "I almost overslept," she said. "My mom said I needed 'one normal night of sleep' but I dreamed about horse thieves and woke up anyway."

Riley managed a small smile. "Welcome to the club."

Dale opened the front door and waved them inside. The three girls followed him into the living room, where the sheriff already sat on an armchair facing the couch. His hat rested on the coffee table, and a folder sat in his lap.

Emma's heart hammered as she sat between Riley and Mia. The couch cushions dipped under their combined weight, and for a moment she focused on that small physical detail just to steady herself.

"Thank you for coming," the sheriff said. "I know you have had a hard few days."

Emma nodded but did not trust herself to speak.

"We appreciate you telling the truth," he continued. "If you had not reported what you saw and found, this would have been much harder to piece together."

Emma forced her voice to work. "Did you find out who he is?"

The sheriff looked at Dale, then back at the girls. "We are close," he said. "Very close. I cannot give names yet, but I can tell you what we have learned."

He opened the folder on his lap. Inside were several photographs: close-ups of bootprints in dirt, tire treads, the broken barn door frame, and the torn glove Dale had shown them before.

"We compared the glove and bootprints with evidence from another case," he said. "The pattern matches someone who has been suspected of moving horses illegally between properties. He has never been caught doing anything serious enough to charge, but he has been seen more than once near auctions and back roads where abandoned animals are found."

Emma felt her heart beating faster. "So he is used to hiding things."

"Yes," the sheriff said. "And he does not work alone. There is an operation behind him. It involves a breeder connected to Pine Hollow and a small ring of buyers and movers."

Riley leaned forward. "So Rusty came from them."

The sheriff nodded. "All of our evidence points that way. The crooked jaw, the markings, the timing of the missing foals in the inspection report. And there was something else."

He reached into the folder and pulled out a printed photograph. It showed a foal standing in a small pen beside a mare. The picture was grainy, taken from a distance, but the white crooked star on the foal's forehead was unmistakable.

"That is Rusty," Mia breathed.

"Taken about a month ago," the sheriff said. "Someone from the inspector's office snapped this while touring a property out near Pine Hollow. It was not part of the official file, but Dr. Huxley requested additional images to compare markings. This one arrived last night."

Emma stared at the photo. Rusty looked smaller, thinner, his eyes duller than they were now. The mare beside him had a strained, tired look as she leaned over her foal.

"He did not look happy," Emma said softly.

"Probably was not," Riley murmured.

"The inspector noted that the foal and mare disappeared before the follow-up visit," the sheriff said. "The owner claimed they were sold to a trainer. No records appear in any of the usual sale barns. That is a red flag."

Emma swallowed. "So they got rid of him quietly."

"That is what we believe," the sheriff said. "And when the story of an abandoned foal found near Saddle Creek started spreading through the grapevine, someone got nervous."

"The intruder," Riley said.

"Yes," the sheriff replied. "He likely panicked that the foal survived and could be traced back to his employer. Returning here was an attempt to remove the evidence before we could connect the dots."

Emma clenched her hands in her lap. "But he failed."

"He did," the sheriff agreed. "In part because of you."

Emma felt a faint warmth beneath the fear. "What happens now?"

"We pursue this lead more aggressively," the sheriff said. "We are working on warrants to search the property and seize any animals in danger. Dr. Huxley will be present to identify medical issues. And as for Rusty, we have enough proof to argue that he was abandoned and mistreated. That strengthens the case that he should not go back there."

Emma looked up quickly. "So he can stay?"

The sheriff's expression softened. "I cannot promise until the paperwork is final. But it is looking positive."

Emma felt some of the tightness in her chest ease. Riley exhaled slowly, and Mia wiped her eyes quickly with her sleeve.

"But," the sheriff continued, "that does not mean we can relax. If this man realizes we are getting close, he may try again. Desperate people make desperate choices."

Emma nodded. The relief mixed with a new kind of worry. "So we still have to be careful."

"Yes," the sheriff said. "Extra security will help. Cameras, reinforced doors, more lighting around the barn. You girls should continue to stay together. Do not go into the woods. Do not approach anyone near the property line you do not recognize. And if you see or hear anything unusual, you call Dale or your aunt and uncle immediately. Understood?"

"Yes," Emma said.

"Understood," Riley and Mia echoed.

The sheriff closed the folder. "One more thing. Dr. Huxley noticed something on Rusty yesterday that might help the investigation and your understanding of where he came from."

Emma frowned. "What do you mean?"

"A scar," the sheriff said. "A small one. On his neck, hidden under the mane. It looked old enough to have healed but recent enough to be related to his past few months. Huxley will show you and explain. It might be painful to hear, but I think you are strong enough now to know."

Emma felt a chill slide down her spine. "What happened to him?"

"That is part of what we are going to find out," the sheriff said. "But we know this much: whatever they did, he survived it. And now he has people on his side."

Dale put a hand on Emma's shoulder. "Come on," he said gently. "Let us go see him."

They walked together toward the barn. The path felt different now, like it was carrying them toward some kind of truth they had been circling around for days without quite touching. The wind picked up slightly, rustling the leaves in the trees. The woods still looked deep and secretive, but the idea that someone might finally have to answer for what they had done to Rusty made them seem a little less powerful.

Dr. Huxley was already in the barn when they arrived, standing beside Rusty's stall with his bag at his feet. Rusty dozed with his head low, ears relaxed, and his breathing steady. When Emma stepped inside, the colt lifted his head and bumped her shoulder gently, as if to remind her that he was there, alive and real and solid.

"I hear you have been busy helping the sheriff," Dr. Huxley said with a small smile.

"We just told him what we saw," Emma answered. "You are the one doing the important part."

"Everyone is doing an important part," he replied. "Even Rusty."

Emma stroked Rusty's neck. "The sheriff said you found a scar."

The vet nodded. "I did. I wanted to show you in a calmer moment. I think understanding it will help you see just how strong this little fellow is."

He parted Rusty's mane gently on the left side of his neck. Beneath the thick hair, Emma saw a faint line of pale skin, no more than two inches long, curving slightly. It was thin but noticeable against the darker coat.

"I missed it at first," Dr. Huxley said. "It had healed well, and the mane covered it. But when I ran my hand along his neck yesterday, he flinched in one particular spot. That made me look closer."

"What caused it?" Emma asked.

"It looks like a rope burn or a halter injury," the vet explained. "Most likely from a too-tight tie or from pulling back in panic while tied to something solid. If a foal fights against that kind of restraint and no one steps in, they can injure themselves badly. He might have been tied somewhere he should not have been."

Emma's stomach twisted. "Like to a fence or a trailer."

"Possibly," Dr. Huxley said. "Or to a rough post in a small holding area. What matters now is that the scar tells us he was restrained and panicked. It fits with the idea that he was handled roughly, perhaps by someone who did not care if he injured himself."

Rusty shifted under Emma's hand, and she felt a tremor move through his muscles. She rubbed the opposite side of his neck gently, trying to give comfort without touching the scar itself.

"He still let us put a halter on him," she said. "He still followed us into the arena."

"That is what makes him remarkable," Dr. Huxley replied. "Even after what he endured, he chose to trust you."

Riley stepped closer to the stall. "Can that scar help connect him to the breeder?"

"It might," the vet said. "If other foals from that property show similar injury patterns, it strengthens the case that this was not an isolated accident. I have already contacted colleagues who have treated horses from that breeder. We will compare notes."

"So all the bad things they did might finally catch up with them," Mia said quietly.

"That is the hope," Dr. Huxley said.

Emma watched Rusty as he lowered his head again, the tension gradually leaving his body as she continued to stroke him. The idea that he had fought against a rope, panicked and desperate, while someone ignored his fear, filled her with a hot surge of anger. But beneath the anger, a different feeling rose.

Pride.

Rusty had survived. He had endured pain and abandonment and fear, and yet here he was, leaning into her hand, choosing to trust anyway.

"He is tougher than he looks," she murmured.

"That he is," Dr. Huxley agreed.

Dale cleared his throat. "There is one more thing you girls should know," he said. "The sheriff will likely confront this breeder soon. If they feel cornered, they might try something drastic, like claiming Rusty or sending someone to argue that he belongs to them."

"They cannot have him," Emma said immediately.

"No, they cannot," Dale said. "Not if we can prove abandonment and harm. But they might not come through official channels. That is why we are staying on alert."

Emma nodded. Her hands had stopped shaking without her noticing. The fear was still there, but it no longer felt like something that owned her. It felt like something she carried alongside something else.

Resolve.

"What can we do?" she asked.

"For now," Dale said, "you keep doing what you have been doing. Care for Rusty. Watch for anything out of place. Stay together. And be ready to act quickly if something happens."

"Act how?" Riley asked.

"By telling us immediately," Dale replied. "You are not responsible for chasing anyone or solving everything. Your job is to notice and report. Leave the confrontation to the adults and the sheriff."

Emma knew he was right, but she also knew that no one could stop her from standing between Rusty and danger if it came to that. She would not charge into the woods alone or chase a stranger across the fields. She had learned that lesson. But if someone stepped into this barn and reached for her foal, she also knew where she would stand.

Right in front of him.

Later that afternoon, as the sun slanted low across the arena and students began to pack up their grooming kits and lead their lesson horses back to their stalls, a patrol car pulled into the drive again. The sheriff stepped out and spoke briefly with Dale near the equipment shed. Emma, Riley, and Mia watched from the barn aisle.

"What do you think he is saying?" Mia whispered.

"Probably telling Dale how the warrant is going," Riley said.

Emma's eyes stayed locked on the two men. At one point, the sheriff pulled out his phone and showed Dale something on the screen. Whatever it was made Dale's eyebrows lift and his mouth tighten.

A moment later, Dale waved the girls over.

"You have good ears," Riley muttered under her breath.

"We listen for a living," Mia replied.

When they reached the men, the sheriff slipped his phone back into his pocket.

"I thought you would want to know," he said, "that the judge approved a full search of the breeder's property. We go out tomorrow. Dr. Huxley will join us. If we find what we expect to find, this whole ring may start to fall apart."

Emma's chest filled with a mix of hope and dread. "Will you tell them about Rusty?"

"We will," the sheriff said. "But not to return him. To add his case to the file. Abandoning him like that will count against them."

"What if they pretend they want him back?" Mia asked. "Like to look like they care."

"That would work against them too," the sheriff replied, his tone calm. "The law does not take nicely to people who only care about animals when they feel cornered."

Riley nodded slowly. "So tomorrow is a big day."

"It is," the sheriff said. "Once we have more, we will be closer to making sure you and your foal are left in peace."

Emma liked the sound of that. Peace. Calm. A barn where the worst thing that happened in the night was a horse kicking a water bucket over.

As the sheriff drove away, Emma stood for a long moment staring at the cloud of dust his tires left behind. The sun was beginning to dip lower, painting the tops of the trees in honey-gold light. Willow grazed quietly in her paddock, her tail swishing lazily at flies. For once, her posture looked relaxed.

"What are you thinking?" Riley asked, coming to stand beside her.

Emma took a breath. "I am thinking tomorrow could change everything."

"For better or worse?" Mia asked, joining them.

"For better," Emma said. She let herself believe it as she said it. "It has to."

They watched the horizon for another moment, then turned back to the barn.

Inside, Rusty was waiting.

He lifted his head and nickered when he saw them, his eyes bright, as if he could sense the shift in the air. Emma stepped into his stall, followed by Riley and Mia.

"We are getting closer," she said softly, resting her forehead against Rusty's. "Soon they will not be able to touch you."

Rusty exhaled a warm breath against her cheek.

He did not know about warrants or legal cases or breeders or intruders.

But he knew one thing.

He was not alone in that stall.

And somewhere beyond the trees and beyond the county road, people who had once treated him as a problem were about to discover that he had become something else entirely.

Evidence.

A living proof that their secrets could not stay buried forever.

As dusk settled over Saddle Creek, and barn lights flicked on one by one, Emma felt the story shift again. They were no longer only defending. They were moving toward the heart of the truth, step by step.

The plot that had once crept like a shadow along the fence line was now standing firmly in the open.

And tomorrow, in the quiet barns and hidden paddocks of a property far from Saddle Creek, that shadow would finally meet the light.

Chapter Eleven

The day the sheriff left for Pine Hollow began like any other, but Emma felt the shift before anything happened. She sensed it in the stillness of the air and the way the horses flicked their ears toward the woods more than usual. Even Rusty pressed closer to her whenever she stepped into his stall. He leaned so heavily against her side that her hip ached, but she could not bring herself to step away.

Dale spent the entire morning strengthening locks around the barn. Fresh boards were laid across the back doors. New padlocks sparkled silver in the sunlight. Floodlights had been installed high on the barn roof and hooked to motion sensors. Everything looked secure, but Emma's nerves stayed tight.

When the sheriff and Dr. Huxley left in the early afternoon to serve the warrant, Emma had watched the patrol car roll down the long gravel lane until the dust cloud faded. Riley and Mia stood on either side of her, silent, the way friends get when words only make everything feel heavier.

"They will find what they need," Riley said, though her voice did not sound entirely certain.

"Yeah," Emma whispered. "I hope so."

The girls spent the next hours helping with chores, sweeping aisles, scrubbing buckets, and exercising Willow in the small round pen. Willow was alert but not on edge. She circled quietly under Emma's guiding voice, her tail loose, her ears flicking back to listen.

"You are doing better today," Emma murmured as Willow came to a halt in front of her. She rubbed the mare's forehead. "You can feel it too, can't you? Something is changing."

By the time the sun dipped low and painted the sky orange, Emma's nerves were tingling again. She felt restless, unable to settle. The sheriff had not yet called with updates. Dale had been pacing between the house and the barn every half hour.

"Let Rusty settle for the night," Dale said as he passed them again. "But keep the barn lights on. I will bring out the portable lanterns for the paddocks too."

Emma nodded. Rusty had already curled up in his stall, his legs tucked under him. She hated to leave him even for a moment, but Dale insisted they eat dinner before dark. She gave Rusty one more rub on his neck.

"I will be right back," she whispered. "Promise."

Rusty's ears shifted as if he understood.

Dinner passed slowly, every tick of the clock stretching Emma's nerves thinner. She tried to eat, but the food felt like a knot in her throat. When Dale finally leaned back and exhaled loudly, Emma nearly jumped out of her chair.

"We go check on the barn soon," he said. "I do not want you girls wandering far, but you can help me give Willow her night feed."

Emma stood so fast her chair scraped loudly across the floor. Riley and Mia followed. The sky outside had deepened to a dusky purple. Fireflies flicked on in small glowing clusters along the grass. Somewhere in the distance, a dog barked.

They walked together toward the barn, the air still and heavy.

Emma clutched the small flashlight Dale handed her, though the floodlights cast bright circles across the barns and paddocks.

When they entered the barn, Willow lifted her head and nickered softly. Rusty stood too, ears pricked, as if sensing something.

Emma stepped inside Rusty's stall and breathed in the warm scent of hay and foal coat. He leaned into her immediately.

"Hey, buddy," she whispered. "You are okay."

Riley spread fresh hay in Storm's stall while Mia checked feed buckets. Dale moved to the tack room to grab a bag of pellets for Willow.

Everything felt peaceful.

Normal.

Almost.

Then Willow froze.

Her entire body stiffened. Her neck arched slightly. Her ears locked on the back doors.

"What is it?" Mia whispered.

Willow's tail flicked once, sharply. She snorted and pawed the ground.

Rusty's head shot up, eyes wide.

Emma stepped back from the stall rail. "What is wrong?"

Riley slowly stepped out into the center aisle. "Something is outside."

A chill threaded through Emma's spine. She clutched the flashlight tighter.

"Dale?" she called quietly.

"I am right here," he answered, stepping back into the main aisle. But when he saw Willow's posture, his expression immediately sharpened.

"Girls," he said, his voice low and urgent. "Stay behind me."

Emma moved Rusty into the far corner of the stall, her heart thudding wildly.

The barn went quiet.

Completely quiet.

The kind of quiet that does not belong on a ranch full of horses.

No night insects.

No distant frogs.

No wind in the leaves.

Nothing.

It was as if the woods were holding their breath.

Then a sound broke the silence.

A single metallic click from outside the back doors.

Emma's breath froze.

Riley hissed, "That is the latch."

Dale strode toward the back doors, but before he reached them, the floodlight above the barn flicked on with a harsh buzz.

A tall shadow appeared just beyond the wood frame.

Emma felt her knees weaken. She grabbed the stall rail to steady herself.

Rusty whimpered, trembling.

The shadow moved closer.

Heavy boots crunched on the gravel. The back door shuddered once, twice, then—

A sharp snap echoed through the barn.

The lock plate bent.

"Dale," Emma whispered.

Dale positioned himself directly between the doors and the aisle. His voice was strong but controlled. "Girls. Stay where you are. If I say run, you run to the house."

Riley swallowed hard. "We are not leaving you."

"You will if I say so," Dale said firmly.

Another snap.

The door hinges strained.

Emma could not move. She stared through the darkness, heart pounding so loudly she could hear it in her ears.

Then the door burst inward.

A tall man stepped into the barn, his silhouette framed by the harsh floodlight. His shoulders were broad, his boots caked in mud. A hood shadowed most of his face, but Emma caught a glimpse of the lower half.

Strong jaw.

Unshaven.

Cold.

He carried a long rope coiled around his arm.

Rusty screamed.

Emma clamped a hand over her mouth, her whole body shaking.

The man stepped forward. "Move," he growled at Dale.

His voice was low, rough, and unmistakably familiar from the night Rusty was found.

Dale did not move. "You are not welcome here."

The man's hand tightened around the rope. "That foal is mine."

"No," Emma said before she could stop herself. She stepped forward, out of Rusty's stall. "He is not."

Riley grabbed her arm, but Emma yanked free.

The intruder's head snapped toward her. She felt his gaze like a physical force, dark and sharp.

"You the girl who found him?" he asked.

Emma's breath caught. She nodded once.

He dropped the rope to his side and took a step toward her.

Dale stepped in front of her instantly. "Stop."

The man sneered. "That foal was supposed to be gone. He is weak. Worthless. He belongs to the breeder, not some little girl."

Emma's heart seared with anger. "He survived because he is strong, not worthless."

He let out a harsh, humorless laugh. "You think you saved him? You made it worse. Now everyone is following me. Looking for things they should not see."

Mia whimpered. Riley shoved her behind the grain bins.

Emma did not move.

The man took another step.

Dale planted his feet. "Turn around. Leave now."

The man lifted the rope. "Move."

"No," Emma said again, louder this time. Something fierce rose inside her, breaking through the fear. "You are not getting Rusty."

The intruder lunged forward.

Rusty screamed again.

And Willow exploded.

The mare shot forward in her stall with a roar of fury Emma had never heard from her before. She reared up high, hooves slamming against her stall door. The barn shook with the force.

Everyone froze.

The man stumbled back.

Willow screamed again, her eyes blazing, ears pinned flat. She struck the stall door so hard the hinges groaned.

Emma realized suddenly what Willow was doing.

She was placing herself between Emma and danger.

The intruder swore and stepped back instinctively. Dale lunged forward and seized the opportunity. He grabbed the man by the arm and shoved him backward. The intruder stumbled into the wall, the rope falling from his grip.

"Riley!" Dale shouted. "Call the sheriff!"

Riley sprinted toward the front of the barn.

The man growled and shoved Dale off. "You have no idea what you are dealing with," he snarled.

Emma found her voice. "I know enough. You hurt him. You abandoned him. And you came back to finish it."

The man's eyes hardened. "That foal was a mistake. I am fixing it."

"I will not let you," Emma said.

The man turned toward her again, fury twisting his expression.

But Willow reared once more with a scream that echoed through the rafters.

Her hooves came down against the stall door with a shuddering crack.

The man flinched and stumbled back again.

Dale seized the moment. He dove forward, grabbing the man's

jacket. The intruder wrenched free and bolted toward the back doors.

Dale lunged after him, but the man slipped through the frame and sprinted out into the dark.

"Get inside!" Dale shouted over his shoulder. "Lock the house! Now!"

Emma, Riley, and Mia ran. Emma reached Rusty's stall and threw her arms around him one last time.

"You are safe," she whispered, breath shaking. "I promise."

Rusty pressed into her chest, his entire body trembling.

Riley grabbed her hand. "Come on!"

Emma tore herself away and followed the girls out of the barn. Willow whinnied behind them, a sharp, protective cry that echoed long after they sprinted across the yard.

They raced toward the farmhouse as floodlights clicked on across the property.

Halfway there, sirens wailed in the distance.

The sheriff was coming.

Emma stumbled onto the porch and looked back at the barn.

The woods were silent.

The intruder was gone.

But he had seen her. Spoken to her. Tried to reach Rusty.

Everything inside Emma shook with fear.

But beneath the terror, something else began to burn.

Resolve.

This time, she knew exactly what she was fighting for.

And she was not backing down.

Tomorrow, things would change.

Tonight had shown one thing clearly:

The man who thought Rusty was worthless was wrong.

The foal had found people who would defend him.

And Emma was done being afraid.

The climax had begun.

Chapter Twelve

For the first time in what felt like a very long time, the woods around Saddle Creek were quiet in a way that did not make Emma's skin prickle.

They were just woods again.

The dark trunks that had once seemed to lean in like listening giants now stood straight and still in the morning sun. Birds hopped along the fence posts. A soft breeze moved through the long grass by the creek. If you did not know what had happened there, you would never guess that a frightened foal had once cried alone in the shadows, or that a man with anger in his eyes had tried to erase his existence.

But Emma knew.

And because she knew, the normal morning sounds felt like a gift someone had wrapped just for her.

She walked down the gravel path from the farmhouse to the barn with her jacket half zipped and hands tucked in the pockets, the cool air brushing her cheeks. Dew clung to the grass, sparkling in the early light. Every inhale carried the scent of hay, damp earth, and the faint sweetness of grain. It smelled like the life she loved, and now it also smelled like something else.

Safety.

The sheriff had called two days after the confrontation in the barn. Emma still remembered the sound of the phone ringing, the way Dale had stepped outside to take the call, and how everyone in the kitchen had gone completely silent until he walked back in.

"They found everything they needed," he had said, eyes tired but shining. "Records. Horses in poor condition. Hidden pens. They are shutting it all down."

Emma had almost dropped her fork. "So that means..."

"It means Rusty was one of the lucky ones," Dale said. "And it means the people who hurt him and others like him will finally have to answer for it."

Now, a week later, the shock had worn off, but the relief had not. It still came in waves when she looked at Rusty or heard Willow's calm breaths at night, washed over her when she remembered the way the intruder had run and how he had not come back.

She reached the barn doors and paused, placing a hand on the smooth worn wood. It no longer felt like the entrance to a battlefield. It felt like a threshold between the world and the place that had become her real home.

Inside, the barn glowed with the soft gold of early light and the warmer glow of hanging lamps. Horses shifted in their stalls, snorted softly, and shook their manes. A radio played quietly from the tack room, some country song about roads and hearts and long rides. Emma smiled.

Rusty's head popped up over his stall door the moment he heard her boots. His ears pricked forward, and he let out a soft, eager nicker.

"There you are," Emma said, her chest loosening. She crossed the aisle and rubbed the white star on his forehead. He leaned against her, bumping her shoulder with more confidence than he had ever shown the first week he was here.

He was stronger now. His ribs no longer showed. His coat shone with good feed and proper care. The hollow look in his eyes had faded, replaced by a brightness that made Emma feel like she had swallowed sunlight.

"Morning, trouble," Riley's voice floated from behind her.

Emma looked over her shoulder and grinned. Riley walked down the aisle with Storm's halter slung over one shoulder and hay bits stuck to her sweater. Her hair was in a loose braid, and her cheeks were pink from the cool air.

"You are not talking to me, are you?" Emma said, pretending to look offended.

"Maybe a little," Riley replied. "But mostly him." She jerked her chin toward Rusty. "He tried to open his stall latch again earlier. I am pretty sure he watched Dale doing it and decided he could do it better."

Emma laughed and scratched Rusty's neck. "You are not allowed to be that smart yet. We just got finished with being constantly terrified for you."

Rusty snorted, which made Riley chuckle.

Mia appeared next, balancing a small bucket in one hand and a clipboard in the other. "Rusty's morning mash, delivered with love and a very professional feeding chart," she announced. "Also, Dale says to remind you that someone has to help him pull out the poles for the big announcement later."

"Big announcement?" Emma asked, taking the bucket.

Mia's eyes widened. "He did not tell you?"

"Apparently not," Emma said.

Riley leaned on the stall door. "He said he wanted all of us there. Staff, riders, and especially you, Emma."

Emma's curiosity grew. "Now I really want to know."

"Finish feeding your spoiled colt and maybe we will find out," Riley said.

Emma rolled her eyes but smiled. She set the bucket down inside Rusty's stall and watched him eat with steady, eager bites. He still checked over his shoulder sometimes, still flinched at sharp noises, but each day the fear loosened its grip a little more.

A lot like her, she realized.

When the chores were finished and the last wheelbarrow had been emptied, the sun had fully climbed into the sky. Dale called everyone to the outdoor arena. Riders, parents, and boarders gathered near the rail. Some sat on the bleachers, others leaned on the fence. Horses dozed in paddocks or watched curiously from the nearest fields.

Emma, Riley, and Mia stood together near the center of the group. Emma shaded her eyes with her hand as Dale stepped into the middle of the arena, his boots quietly crunching on the sand.

He looked comfortable and at home there, as he always did. A baseball cap shaded his brow, and his plaid shirt sleeves were rolled up to his elbows. The breeze tugged lightly at the ends of his hair.

"Thank you all for coming out," he called. His voice carried easily across the ring. "I know we have had a rough patch lately. A lot of long nights, a lot of worry. But I wanted to bring everyone together today for two reasons."

Emma's pulse quickened.

"First," Dale continued, "to tell you that the investigation we have all been worried about is finally meeting justice. The breeder responsible for abandoning Rusty, and for mistreating other horses, is being charged. Animals are being moved to safe homes, and the operation will not be continuing."

A round of quiet applause rippled through the crowd. Some of the adults nodded with visible relief. Dr. Huxley stood near the rail, his arms folded, a small smile on his face.

Emma felt a swell of emotion. She glanced at Riley and Mia. Both girls were grinning.

"Second," Dale said, and his voice took on a slightly different tone. Lighter. Warmer. "I wanted to mark the end of this hard chapter with something new. Something exciting. Something that shows the future of Saddle Creek is not just about surviving. It is about growing."

He paused for a moment, letting the words settle.

"Starting this fall," he said, "Saddle Creek Ranch will be launching its own in-house **medal class series**."

A wave of murmurs swept through the riders.

"A medal class?" a teen rider from the advanced group whispered behind Emma. "Here?"

Emma's heart jumped. She had heard about medal classes. She had seen them online, watched videos of older riders guiding tall, gleaming horses over precise, beautiful courses. Medal classes were about more than just jumps. They were about style, precision, partnership. They were the kind of event riders talked about in low, excited voices.

Dale went on, "We will host a series of schooling medal rounds here at Saddle Creek over the next few months, leading up to a fall final. Courses will be more technical. Expectations a bit higher. This is a chance for our riders to grow not just as competitors, but as partners with their horses."

Riley let out a low whistle. "Whoa."

Mia gripped her clipboard tighter. "That sounds intense. And cool. Mostly cool. Also scary."

Emma's mind raced. A medal class. Here. On the same arena sand where she had once just tried to keep Willow trotting in a circle without drifting toward the fence.

Dale smiled. "We will have divisions for different levels. Some of you are already strong enough to start schooling medal-type courses. Some of you will be ready by the end of summer. And some of you will help just by learning how a show like this runs, because horses need all kinds of people around them, not just riders in the ring."

Emma felt a flutter of something in her chest. Interest. Excitement. And something deeper.

Could she be one of those riders?

Dale's eyes swept the crowd and landed, very briefly, on her. The look was not long. But it was enough.

He believes I can, she thought, feeling her throat tighten.

"We are also expanding our schooling show calendar," he said. "Including bringing in a few guest riders and clinicians to raise the level here and push us all to learn more."

"Guest riders?" Mia whispered.

Riley arched an eyebrow. "You know what that means."

Emma swallowed. "New people."

"New riders," Riley corrected. "New competition."

Her voice held no real bitterness, just anticipation.

Dale finished the announcement with details about dates, sign-up sheets, and a promise that more information would be posted on the barn bulletin board. People began buzzing with questions and excitement as the crowd broke apart.

"That was huge," Mia said as they walked back toward the barn. "Medal classes. Guests. Clinics. It is like Saddle Creek is leveling up."

"About time," Riley said, though she smiled as she said it. "I am ready for harder courses."

Emma walked quietly for a moment, absorbing everything. Harder courses meant more pressure. More eyes. More chances to fail. Part of her flinched at the thought. But another part of her, the part that had run for help in the dark, that had stood up to a man who called her foal worthless, that had helped Rusty take his first brave circle around the arena, felt something else.

Readiness.

"What about you?" Riley asked, bumping Emma's shoulder lightly. "You going to go for it? The medal class?"

Emma hesitated. "I do not know if I am good enough."

"You are not," Riley said immediately.

Emma stared at her. "Wow. Thanks."

Riley snorted. "Let me finish. You are not good enough... yet. But you could be. That is what these classes are for. To get better."

Mia nodded eagerly. "You have already changed so much. Look at how you ride Willow now. You are not the same girl who showed up here in Book One, you know."

Emma smiled despite herself. "You realize you just said 'Book One' like our lives are a series on a shelf."

"Is it not?" Mia grinned.

Riley rolled her eyes affectionately. "Regardless of what shelf we are on, I think you should go for it. It will not be easy. But you are not the kind of person who backs off just because something is scary."

Emma looked down at her hands. She remembered how they had shaken when she first found Rusty. How they had trembled when she watched the intruder step into the barn. How, even through the fear, she had stepped forward anyway.

Maybe I am not that girl anymore, she thought. At least, not only that girl.

"I will think about it," she said.

"You better do more than think," Riley replied. "You better start practicing."

They reached the barn, and the familiar scents and sounds wrapped around Emma like a hug. She walked to Rusty's stall, where the foal stood dozing in the sunshine slanting through the window.

"We are getting medal classes," she told him, resting a hand on his neck. "Can you believe it?"

Rusty opened one eye and blinked at her as if to say that as long as there were snacks involved, he could handle anything.

Later that afternoon, after chores and a short ride on Willow, Emma stopped near the bulletin board outside the tack room. Dale had already pinned up a neat sheet of paper with the words:

SADDLE CREEK MEDAL SERIES

Sign-ups open next week

Divisions: Green Rider, Novice, Intermediate, Open

Schooling dates listed below

Handwriting had started to appear along the margins where riders had added jokes and questions.

"Do we get ribbons?"

"Will Knightfall be used?"

"Do we need show clothes?"

"Is there a cool trophy?"

Mia pointed at one note that made her giggle. "Look. 'Will there be snacks in the viewing area.' That has to be Sara."

Riley snorted. "Of course it is Sara."

Emma leaned closer to the list of possible horses Dale had written in the corner. Willow's name was there. So was Storm's. So was Knightfall's.

Knightfall was one of the most striking geldings at Saddle Creek, tall and black with a graceful neck and a bold jump. He had carried more than one rider through their first real course, ears pricked, hooves striking the ground with confident rhythm.

"Knightfall is on the list," Emma said.

"He should be," Riley replied. "He is a rock star."

As if summoned, Knightfall stuck his head out of his stall and snorted. They laughed.

They were still standing there when Dale came up behind them, wiping his hands on a towel.

"Knights on the list," he confirmed. "But we will see how he feels about that when we start schooling."

"What does that mean?" Emma asked.

"He has been a little looky at the new fillers in the arena," Dale said. "Nothing serious. Just big feelings. A few refusals. He will need confident riders if he is going to step into medal-level courses."

Riley's eyes lit up. "I volunteer."

"You might get your wish," Dale said. "But we will pair horses and riders carefully."

As he walked away, Emma felt a small flicker of nerves. Confident riders. That phrase still made her shrink a little inside.

Not yet, she thought. But maybe soon.

The rest of the day slipped by in small, normal moments that felt precious because of how close they had come to losing them.

Cleaning tack. Laughing at Mia when she dropped a grooming brush and Storm nudged it back to her. Watching Willow nap in a patch of sunlight. Scratching Rusty's favorite itchy spots until he leaned against her like a big dog.

As the sun began to sink, painting the sky with streaks of pink and gold, Emma and Riley sat on the fence overlooking the arena. The jumps were still set low from earlier lessons. Someone had left a pattern of bright blue and white poles in one corner, and the sight of them sent a small thrill through Emma.

"You know what I like about today?" Riley said.

"What?" Emma asked.

"That the scariest thing we talked about was whether or not we are ready to jump higher," Riley replied. "Not whether someone is going to break into the barn."

Emma smiled softly. "Yeah. Me too."

Mia joined them, climbing up onto the fence rail with a little huff. "My mom says I can sign up for the Green Rider division," she announced. "I told her I might die of nerves. She said that is what practice is for."

Riley grinned. "Your mom is not wrong."

Emma swung her boots gently against the bottom rail. "Do you ever think about how different we are from when we first came here?"

"All the time," Mia said. "I used to think trot poles were terrifying. Now I am considering medal courses. That is insane."

"You are the same you," Riley said. "Just with more tools."

Emma looked out over the arena. The sand glowed softly in the last light. Beyond it, the woods stood quiet, but now they looked like the backdrop to a story that had been told, not one that was still unfolding.

Her fear had not vanished completely. But it no longer defined her. It sat beside something else now.

Anticipation.

A truck engine rumbled in the distance.

Emma turned her head. A long, white horse trailer rolled slowly up the driveway, tires crunching over gravel. The late sunlight reflected off its sides, making it hard to see at first.

"Is someone getting picked up?" Mia asked.

"There is no pick-up scheduled today," Riley said, frowning. "Not that I heard."

The trailer pulled to a stop near the parking area. The truck door opened, and a man climbed out, stretching his back. He walked toward the trailer's side door.

Dale stepped out of the barn office and headed toward him. The two men shook hands. They exchanged a few words none of the girls could hear.

Emma's heart started to thump.

"Do you think..." she began.

"Guest rider," Riley said. "It has to be."

"Or a boarder?" Mia added. "Or both?"

The trailer door creaked open. A ramp was lowered with a soft thud. The three girls leaned forward on the fence without meaning to.

A dark bay horse stepped carefully down the ramp, ears pricked, neck arched. Its coat gleamed even under the dust of travel, and its eyes were bright and alert. A figure followed, one hand on the horse's lead rope.

He was about their age. Slightly taller than Emma, with messy brown hair and a worn baseball cap turned backward on his head. Even from a distance, Emma could tell he moved like someone who was used to being around horses. Easy. Confident. Comfortable.

He patted the bay's neck, glanced around the ranch, and said something to Dale that made them both smile.

"Called it," Riley said softly. There was no jealousy in her voice yet, only curiosity sharpened by competitiveness. "New rider."

Mia's eyes were big. "He looks like he knows what he is doing."

Emma's heart beat strangely fast. She could not hear his voice from where they sat, but she watched the way he moved, the way the bay horse stepped beside him without crowding or lagging, the way he seemed to take in the jumps and the arena with a practiced eye.

"Do you think he is here for the medal series?" Mia asked.

"I think he is here for more than that," Riley replied quietly. "You can just tell."

Emma did not say anything. She watched as the boy led the horse toward the barn. As he passed the arena, he looked up and saw the three girls on the fence. For a fraction of a second, their eyes met.

He gave a small nod. Not shy. Not cocky. Just sure.

Emma nodded back, her stomach flipping in a way that had nothing to do with fear this time.

Riley hopped off the fence rail. "Well," she said, dusting off her jeans. "This is going to be interesting."

Mia slid down after her. "Very."

Emma stayed on the fence for another heartbeat, watching the boy and the bay disappear into the barn. The last light of evening slid along the rails of the medal jumps, turning the paint to fire.

She thought about Rusty, safe in his stall. About Willow, who had stood between her and danger. About the woods that had tried to scare her away and had failed.

She had already faced the kind of fear that made your hands shake and your knees want to give out. What was a few higher fences compared to that?

Her heart steadied.

"I think," she said softly, more to herself than to anyone else, "that I am ready."

Ready for harder courses.

Ready for louder shows.

Ready for new riders who might challenge everything she thought she knew about Saddle Creek.

She hopped down from the fence and followed her friends toward the barn.

Behind her, the arena stood quiet, but the lines of jumps and poles seemed to hum with possibilities.

The danger in the woods had passed.

The pressure in the ring was just beginning.

And somewhere inside the barn, a new horse and a new rider were making their first impressions on Saddle Creek.

Emma had no way of knowing yet that the next time they all entered that arena together, the biggest risk she would face would not be a shadow in the trees.

It would be the question every rider has to answer sooner or later.

When the rivals rise, who will you be?

She squared her shoulders and stepped inside.

Whatever the answer was, she would find it in the air above a jump, in the rhythm of hooves on the sand, and in the friends who rode at her side.

The ranch was ready.

So was she.

From Saddle Creek to You

If you are reading this page, it means you stayed with Emma, Rusty, Riley, Mia, Willow, and all of Saddle Creek through the hardest and bravest chapter of their lives. Thank you for riding with them and for caring about a small foal with a crooked star who needed someone to see him, protect him, and believe he deserved more.

And now that Rusty is safe and the shadows have lifted, you might think the next chapter at Saddle Creek would be calm.

But that is the thing about horse life.

Peace never stays still for too long.

Because danger is not the only thing that can shake a ranch.

Sometimes change rides in on four strong hooves and a confident smile... and suddenly everything becomes a little more complicated.

In the very next book in the Saddle Creek Riders series, Emma discovers that surviving fear is one kind of courage.

But stepping into the arena, with eyes watching and riders competing, takes a different kind entirely.

Saddle Creek is launching its very first **medal class series**, and excitement travels through the barn like a spark catching dry grass.

But excitement does not show up alone.

Pressure arrives with it.

So does ambition.

And rivalry.

When a new boy rider steps off a trailer with a polished bay horse and a reputation that whispers ahead of him, the balance at Saddle Creek shifts. Knightfall refuses a jump he has always taken. Rumors begin swirling in corners of the barn aisle. Long friendships bend under the weight of new competition. And the warm-up ring becomes a place where confidence can rise or shatter in a heartbeat.

Emma will face choices she has never had to make before.

Friendships will stretch and egos will flare.

Someone will push too far.

And one dangerous change to a jump might even put a rider in real jeopardy. Through it all, Emma will begin to discover who she is becoming... not just as a rider, but as a teammate, a competitor, and a friend.

So if you are ready for a season of big fences, big feelings, and even bigger rivalries, saddle up for the next ride.

Book Three is waiting in the arena dust and the echo of hooves on the schooling ring.

Saddle Creek Riders - Book 3: Rival Riders Rising

See you at the first jump.

Warm wishes and barn-aisle magic,

Wren Willowbrook

www.ingramcontent.com/pod-product-compliance
Lightning Source LLC
Chambersburg PA
CBHW071838190726
48292CB00005B/1809